Stories for Seven-Ye

At seven most children have reached an age when they are eager for all the stories they can read or hear. They are happy, too, to be delighted by the same tales over and over again. Now is the time to introduce them to the whole range of folk and fairy tale – and to tales from classical mythology. Here is a rich collection of the stories that every child should grow up with. There are folk tales from Grimm and elsewhere, such as *The Three Sillies*, and *Rumpelstiltskin*; there are retellings of the stories of Persephone and King Midas of the Golden Touch; there are tales from Andersen – *The Emperor's New Clothes* and *The Ugly Duckling*; and there are stories from writers of our own century worthy to be read alongside these tried and trusted favourites – Kipling's *The Elephant's Child*, for instance, and V. H. Drummond's *The Flying Postman*.

Seven is a wonderful age and here is a book to add to the wonder. The celebrated compilers have added a special 'Word to the Storyteller' for all those with the enviable task of reading these stories to their children, nieces, nephews or friends.

Sara and Stephen Corrin have together produced a large number of widely loved children's books. Sara, born within the sound of Bow Bells, has always loved sharing stories with child listeners. As a teacher she became known as the story-teller, and now she tells stories up and down the country, especially in children's libraries. She has made the subject of children's responses to literature one of her main studies, and until her retirement was a senior lecturer at a College of Education, specializing in child development. Stephen, brought up on a mixed diet of the *Gem*, the *Magnet*, the Bible, cricket and Beethoven quartets, now spends his time reviewing, writing stories and translating from four languages into English.

Stories for Seven-Year-Olds

and other young readers

EDITED BY

SARA & STEPHEN CORRIN

Illustrated by Shirley Hughes

Puffin Books

in association with Faber & Faber

PUFFIN BOOKS

Published by the Penguin Group
27 Wrights Lane, London w8 5tz, England
Viking Penguin Inc., 40 West 2rd Street, New York, New York 10010, USA
Penguin Books Australia Ltd, Ringwood, Victoria, Australia
Penguin Books Canada Ltd, 2801 John Street, Markham, Ontario, Canada l3r 1b4
Penguin Books (NZ) Ltd, 182–190 Wairau Road, Auckland 10, New Zealand

Penguin Books Ltd, Registered Offices: Harmondsworth, Middlesex, England

This collection (with six more stories) first published by Faber & Faber Ltd 1964
Published in Puffin Books 1976

20

Made and printed in Great Britain by
Richard Clay Ltd, Bungay, Suffolk
Set in Monotype Baskerville

Contents

5

Contents

A Word to the Story-teller

Can stories really be so rigidly classified as to justify the title *Stories for Seven-Year-Olds*? Most teachers will say that they can, which does not imply, of course, that the same stories will not be of interest to other age groups. It means simply that every age has differing emotional and intellectual requirements and that there are some stories very much more suited than others to meet these requirements. Each age-range – and each child within this range – will draw from the story at different levels, according to need; so that in a class of forty seven-year-olds one is catering for forty individuals at forty different levels. And yet the whole class will sit entranced, linked by some magic spell.

Most of the stories in this volume are traditional, but we have included three of Hans Andersen's tales and three belonging to this century. The collection has been tried out and proved its worth with classes of seven-year-olds – as well as with individual children. It will help, of course, if the teacher reads them in such a way as to convey her own enthusiasm for them to the child. This goes for the parent, too, as well as for the aunt or elder sister. The story-teller should not be afraid of adding a little trimming here and there, for these stories are highly condensed affairs. Sometimes a word or phrase may be adapted to suit the capacity or temperament of the particular listener. And above all, the story-teller must not fight shy of dramatizing – dramatic tension is one thing which all young people find irresistible. All this is safely within the story-telling tradition, for over the many years that traditional tales have been handed down they have been added to and embellished in all sorts of ways. But never, of course, beyond recognition. The basic themes remain; we find them appearing in various guises in all parts of the world.

Editor's Note:

Inevitably, with collections of short stories, anthologizers settle on the same outstanding examples and, because of this, the following stories have been dropped from Sara and Stephen Corrin's *Stories for Seven-Year-Olds*, as they appear in other Puffin collections: *Lazy John* (trad.), *The Husband Who Was to Mind the House* (P. C. Asbjornsen), *The Wolf and the Seven Little Kids* (Wanda Gág), *The Golden Goose* (Grimm), *The Sneezing Donkey* (trad.) and *The Princess on the Pea* (Hans Andersen).

However, because of their outstanding merit and because it is felt that the book would be 'robbed of its fire and gold' without them, we have retained *The Twelve Dancing Princesses* (Grimm), *The Golden Touch* (Nathaniel Hawthorne), *East of the Sun and West of the Moon* (Gwyn Jones) and *Baba Yaga and the Little Girl with the Kind Heart* (Arthur Ransome), even though they occur in other Puffins.

The Tinder Box

A soldier came marching away along the high road. One! two! One! two! He had his knapsack on his back and a sword at his side, for he had been in the wars, and now he was off home. Well, he met an old witch on the high road. She was ugly! Her lower lip hung right down on her chest. Said she, 'Good evening, Soldier! What a fine sword, and what a big knapsack you've got! You are a proper soldier. Now you shall get as much money as you care to have.'

'Much obliged to you, old Witch,' said the soldier.

'Do you see that tree?' said the witch, pointing to the tree that stood just by them. 'It's quite hollow inside. You climb up to the top of it, and you'll see a hole that you can let yourself slide down and get right to the bottom of the tree. I'll tie a rope round your waist so as I can hoist you up again when you call to me.'

'Well, what am I to do at the bottom of the tree?' asked the soldier.

'Get money,' said the witch. 'You must know that when you get down to the bottom of the tree you'll be in a long passage. It's quite light, there are more than a hundred lamps burning. There you'll see three doors: you can open them, the keys are in them. If you go into the first room, there you'll see in the middle of the floor a big chest, and on it there sits a dog. He's got a pair of eyes as big as a couple of teacups, but you needn't mind that. I'll give you my blue check apron. You can spread it out on the floor, and then go straight up and pick up the dog and put him on the apron. Open the chest and take as many pence as you like. They're all copper; but if you'd rather have silver, you must go into the next room. There sits a dog who's got a pair of eyes as big as millwheels, but you needn't mind about that; put him on my apron and take the money. But if, on the other hand, you'd like gold, you can get that too, and as much of it as you can carry, if you go into the third room. Only the dog that sits on the chest there has two eyes, each of 'em as big as the Round Tower. He's a dog and a half, I can tell you. But you needn't mind that. Just put him on my apron, he'll do nothing to you, and take as much gold out of the chest as you like.'

'That's not so bad,' said the soldier, 'but what am I to give you, old Witch? For of course you'll be wanting something too, I suppose?'

'No,' said the witch, 'I don't want a single penny. You need only bring me an old tinder box which my granny left behind by mistake the last time she was down there.'

'Right! Let's have the rope round me,' said the soldier.

'Here you are!' said the witch, 'and here's my blue check apron.'

So the soldier climbed up the tree and let himself

plump down into the hole, and there he was, as the witch had said, down in the big passage where all the hundreds of lamps were burning.

Then he opened the first door. Lor! there sat the dog with eyes as big as teacups, and stared at him.

'You're a nice sort of chap!' said the soldier, and put him on the apron and took as many copper pence as he could carry in his pocket, shut the chest, put the dog on the top again and went into the second room. Gracious! There sat the dog with eyes as big as mill-wheels.

'You shouldn't look at me so hard!' said the soldier. 'You might injure your eyesight!' Then he put the dog on the witch's apron; but when he saw the heaps of silver money in the chest, he threw away all the copper money he had got and filled his pocket and his knapsack with nothing but silver. Then he went into the third room. No, now, that was awful! The dog there really had two eyes as big as the Round Tower, and they went round and round in his head like wheels.

'Good evening!' said the soldier, and saluted, for such a dog he never had seen before. But after looking at him for a bit he thought perhaps that would do, and lifted him down on to the floor and opened the chest. Mercy on me, what a lot of gold there was! Enough to pay for all Copenhagen and the cakewoman's sugar pigs, and all the tin soldiers and whips and rocking-horses there were in the whole world. There was money there right enough! So the soldier threw away all the silver shillings he had filled his pockets and his knapsack with, and took gold instead; till all his pockets and his knapsack and his cap and his boots got filled up so that he could hardly walk. Now he had got some money! He put the dog back on the chest, slammed the door and then shouted up through the tree:

'Pull me up now, old Witch!'

'Have you got the tinder box?' asked the witch.

'That's true!' said the soldier. 'I'd clean forgotten it.' So he went and got it. The witch pulled him up and there he was back again on the high road with his pockets and boots and knapsack and cap full of money.

'What do you want with the tinder box?' asked the soldier.

'That's got nothing to do with you!' said the witch. 'You've got your money all right. Just give me the tinder box.'

'Fiddlesticks!' said the soldier. 'You tell me straight off what you mean to do with it, or I'll out with my sword and cut your head off.'

'No!' said the witch.

So the soldier cut her head off. There she lay! But he tied up all his money in her apron and put it on his shoulder in a bundle, shoved the tinder box into his pocket and went straight to the town.

It was a splendid town, and into the finest hotel he went, and ordered the very best rooms and the dishes he liked best, for he was rich, now that he had all that money.

The servant who had to clean his boots certainly thought they were very funny old boots for such a rich gentleman to have; but he hadn't bought any new ones yet. Next day he got boots to walk in and clothes of the smartest. The soldier was now become a fine gentleman, and they told him about all the splendid things that were in their town, and about their King, and what a pretty princess his daughter was.

'Where can one get a sight of her?' the soldier asked.

'Oh, she can't be seen at all,' they all said. 'She lives in a big copper castle with lots of walls and towers round it. Nobody but the King dares go in and out to her, for it's been foretold that she'll be married to a quite common soldier, and the King can't have that!'

'Well, I'd like enough to see her,' thought the soldier; but he couldn't anyhow get leave to do so.

Well, he lived a very merry life, went to the play,

drove in the royal gardens, and gave a lot of money to the poor, and that was a nice thing to do; he knew well enough from old times how horrid it was not to have a penny-piece. He was well off now, and had smart clothes and made a number of friends, who all said he was a good sort and a real gentleman, which pleased the soldier very much. But as every day he laid out money and got none at all back, the end of it was that he had no more than twopence left, and so he had to shift out of the nice rooms where he had lodged, up into a tiny little garret right under the roof, and clean his boots for himself and mend them with a darning-needle; and none of his friends came to see him, because there were so many stairs to climb.

One evening it was quite dark, and he couldn't even buy himself a candle. But just then he remembered that there was a little stump of one in the tinder box he had got from the hollow tree where the witch had helped him down. He got out the tinder box and the stump of candle, and just as he struck it and the spark flew out of the flint, the door sprang open, and the dog that had eyes as big as teacups, whom he had seen down under the tree, stood before him and said: 'What are my lord's orders?'

'What's this?' said the soldier, 'why, this is a jolly tinder box. Can I get whatever I want like this? Get me some money,' said he to the dog, and pop! he was back again with a big bag full of coppers in his mouth. Now the soldier saw what a lovely tinder box this was. If he struck once, the dog came that sat on the chest with the copper money, if he struck twice the one that

14

had the silver came, and if he struck three times the
one that had the gold. The soldier moved back now
into the nice rooms, got into the smart clothes, and at
once all his friends recognized him, and were very
fond of him indeed.

One day he started thinking to himself: 'It's a rum
thing, so it is, that one can't get a sight of the Princess.
They all say she's very pretty, but what's the use of
that if she's got to stay all the time inside that big
copper castle with all the towers? Can't I anyhow get
a sight of her? Where's that tinder box?' So he struck
a light, and pop! here comes the dog with the eyes as
big as teacups. 'I know it's the middle of the night,'
said the soldier, 'all the same, I should dearly like to
see the Princess, if it was only for a minute.' The dog
was off through the door at once, and before the soldier
had time to think, here he was again with the Princess:
she was sitting on the dog's back, asleep, and she was
so pretty, anybody could see she was a real Princess.
The soldier couldn't help it, he had to kiss her, for he
was a genuine soldier. Then the dog ran back again
with the Princess. But when it was morning, and the
King and Queen were pouring out their tea, the
Princess said she had had such a funny dream that
night about a dog and a soldier! She had ridden on the
dog, and the soldier had kissed her.

'Upon my word, that's a nice story!' said the
Queen.

One of the Court ladies had to watch at the Princess's bedside the next night, to see if it really was a
dream, or what else it might be.

The soldier longed dreadfully to see the beautiful Princess again: so the dog came in the night and took her and raced off as hard as he could. But the old lady-in-waiting put on water boots and ran after him just as fast, and when she saw them disappear into a big house she thought: 'Now I know where it is,' and she drew a large cross on the door with a bit of chalk. Then she went home and got into bed, and the dog came back too, with the Princess. But when he saw there was a cross drawn on the door where the soldier lived, he, too, took a bit of chalk and put crosses on all the doors in the whole town; and that was clever of him, for now the lady-in-waiting couldn't find the right door, since there was a cross on every one of them.

Early in the morning the King and Queen and the old lady-in-waiting and all the officials came out to see where it was that the Princess had been. 'Here it is!' said the King, when he saw the first door with a cross on it. 'No, it's here, my darling husband,' said the Queen who spied the next door with a cross on it.

'But here's one, and there's one!' said everybody. Wherever they looked there were crosses on the doors, so they could see it was no use searching.

The Queen, however, was a very clever woman who knew more than how to drive a coach. She took her large gold scissors and clipped a piece of silk into bits, and then made a pretty little bag; this she filled with fine buckwheat flour, tied it to the Princess's back, and when that was done, she cut a little hole in the bag so that the flour could run out all along the way where the Princess went.

At night the dog came again and took the Princess on his back and ran off with her to the soldier, who was very fond of her and would dearly have liked to be a prince, so as to have her for his wife.

The dog never noticed the flour running out all the way from the castle to the soldier's window, where he used to run up the wall with the Princess. So in the morning the King and Queen could see plain enough where their daughter had disappeared to, and they took the soldier and put him in the lock-up.

There he sat. Ugh! how dark and dismal it was; and then they said to him: 'Tomorrow you're to be hanged.' It wasn't amusing to be told that; and he'd left his tinder box behind at the hotel. Next morning he could see, through the iron bars of the little window, the people hurrying out of the town to see him hanged. He heard the drums and saw the soldiers march off. Everybody was on the move; among them a shoemaker's boy with a leather apron and slippers, going at such a galloping pace that one of his slippers flew off right against the wall where the soldier sat peering out between the iron bars.

'Hi! you shoemaker's boy, you needn't be in such a hurry,' said the soldier to him; 'nothing'll happen before I come there, but if you don't mind running to the place I lived at and fetching me my tinder box, you shall have fourpence; only you must put your best foot foremost.' The shoemaker's boy wanted the fourpence, so he darted off to get the tinder box, and gave it to the soldier, and – now we shall hear what happened!

Outside the town a great gallows had been built, and around it stood the soldiers and many hundred thousands of people. The King and Queen sat on a splendid throne straight opposite the Judge and the whole Privy Council.

The soldier was already on the ladder, but just as they were going to put the rope round his neck, he said that as a criminal was always allowed, before he underwent his punishment, to have one innocent wish granted him, he would dearly like to smoke one pipe of tobacco: it would be the last pipe he smoked in this world. The King wouldn't say no to this, so the soldier took out his tinder box and struck a light. One! two! three! and there were all the dogs; the one with eyes as big as teacups, the one with eyes like mill-wheels, and the one with eyes as big as the Round Tower.

'Help me now, so I shan't be hanged,' said the soldier; and the dogs dashed at the judges, and all the council; took one by the legs and another by the nose and threw them yards and yards up in the air, so that they tumbled down and were broken all to bits.

'I won't!' said the King; but the biggest dog took him and the Queen too, and threw them after all the rest. Then the soldiers took fright, and all the people called out: 'Dear good soldier, you shall be our King and have the lovely Princess.' So they put the soldier into the King's coach, and all three dogs danced in front and shouted 'Hurrah!' and the boys whistled on their fingers, and the soldiers presented arms. The Princess was brought out of the copper castle and made Queen, and very much pleased she was. The wedding lasted eight days, and the dogs sat at table and made great eyes.

Rumpelstiltskin

There was once a poor miller who had a very beautiful daughter. So proud was he of this daughter and so very vain that one day he told the King of his country that she was able to spin straw into pure gold thread. Now the King was very excited on hearing this and ordered that she appear before him immediately.

So the miller brought his daughter before the King, who led her to a room full of straw and told her that she must spin it all into pure gold thread by the next morning. 'If you fail,' he said, 'you will have your head chopped off. But if you succeed you will marry my son.' Whereupon he went out and locked the door after him.

Left alone, the maiden began to weep. She knew full well she could never perform such an impossible task. Then all of a sudden the window flew wide open and there appeared before her an ugly little dwarf.

'Why do you weep?' he asked.

'I weep because I have to spin all this straw into pure gold thread before morning. And if I fail, my head will be chopped off.'

'What will you give me if I do it for you?' asked the little dwarf.

'I could give you my beautiful necklace,' replied the maiden.

'Very well then,' said he and he merrily set to work.

In next to no time he had spun all the straw into pure gold thread. Then he vanished into thin air.

The next morning when the King arrived he rubbed his hands in glee at the sight of all the gold. But his heart grew greedy for more and he told the maiden that tonight yet another roomful of straw must be spun into gold.' 'If you fail,' said he, 'you will have your head chopped off.'

No sooner had he left, with the door bolted behind him, than again the window suddenly flew open and again the same ugly little dwarf appeared before the weeping maiden.

'Why do you weep?' he asked.

'I weep because the King has ordered yet another roomful of straw to be spun into gold before morning,' she replied. 'And if I fail I will have my head chopped off.'

'What will you give me this time if I do it for you?' asked the ugly little dwarf.

'I could give you the ring on my finger,' she answered.

'Very well, then,' quoth he and once more he merrily set to work and in next to no time he had spun all the straw into pure gold thread. Then he vanished into thin air.

On the morrow when the King arrived and saw the glistening gold he rubbed his hands in glee.

'If I could have yet one more roomful of gold thread, I should be the richest King in the whole wide world,' thought he. Then he led the girl to a third room full of straw and bade her spin it all into gold thread before morning. 'If you fail,' he warned her, 'you will have your head chopped off. But if you succeed you will marry the Prince, my son.' And he left and locked the door.

Suddenly the windows blew open and there appeared before her the same ugly little dwarf.

'Wherefore do you weep?' he asked.

'I weep because the King has ordered me to spin yet a third roomful of straw into gold thread,' said she.

'What will you give me if I do it for you?' he asked.

'Alas,' said she. 'I have nothing.'

'Then you must make me this promise,' said he. 'If you become Queen you must give me your first child.'

'That may never happen,' thought the maiden. So she promised what he asked. And in next to no time

the little dwarf had spun all the straw into gold thread.
Then he vanished into thin air.

This time when the King appeared the next morning he declared that the maiden should marry his son
and the wedding was celebrated that very day.

Not long after the King died and the Prince and his
wife became King and Queen. Soon a baby was born
to the Queen – such a beautiful baby that as he grew
he became more and more beloved by all around. He
was the darling of his mother and indeed of all the
court.

One night when the Queen lay sleeping with her
little son, suddenly the windows blew open and there
appeared in her room the same ugly little dwarf.

The Queen awoke in terror and remembered her
dread promise.

'I have come to claim your son,' cried the ugly little
dwarf.

'No, not my darling son!' she cried, pressing him to
her breast. 'I will give you all the riches of my kingdom but please, you cannot take my darling son!'

'I do not want your treasures. I want your son,'
cried the ugly little dwarf.

But the Queen wept so pitifully that at last the
dwarf said: 'I will give you three days' grace. Each
evening I will come and ask you to guess my name. If
by the third evening you have not guessed my name,
the baby must come with me.'

The poor Queen summoned all her courtiers and
bade them seek in all four corners of her kingdom to
bring her all the strange names they could find.

When the dwarf came next evening he was grinning away to himself.

'Well, Madam,' he said. 'Have you found my name?'

'Is it Murgatropp?' asked she.

'No!' he shrieked.

'Pugglewick?' she said.

'No!'

'Grossletoes?'

'No!'

'Hipplewhistle?'

'No!'

'Hagglecrockle?'

'No!'

'Bandylegs?'

'No!'

'Devilpickle?'

'No!'

'Cragglewitch?'

'No,' he said, 'and that's all for tonight.' And he vanished into thin air.

The Queen in despair again dispatched her courtiers to all parts of her kingdom and again they came back with the strangest names they could find. But, alas, when the dwarf appeared, to each name he shrieked a terrible 'No'. 'Tomorrow,' he cried, 'is your last chance.' And he vanished into thin air.

This time, however, when her courtiers spread far and wide to the farthest corners of her kingdom, there came one in haste back to the Queen and cried: 'Your Majesty, as I travelled over the mountains, down in the valley I espied a cave where a bright fire was burning. And round the fire a little dwarf was dancing. And as he danced he clapped his hands and sang these words:

> ' *"Merrily the feast I'll make*
> *Today I'll brew, tomorrow bake*
> *Merrily I'll dance and sing*
> *For next day will a stranger bring*
> *Little can she guess, poor dame*
> *That Rumpelstiltskin is my name."* '

The Queen jumped for joy and how happy everybody was. And that evening when the window blew open and the little dwarf appeared, the Queen was ready for him.

But first she pretended she had not guessed his secret.

'Is your name – Muddlenose?'

'No!'

'Is your name ... Screechheat?'

'No!'

'Is your name ... Shingletop?'

'No!'

'Is your name ... Bossleblackentop?'

'No!'

'Is your name ... Shimmerhacklesnout?'

'No,' shrieked the dwarf. 'You have one more guess.'

'Is your – name—

RUMPELSTILTSKIN!'

When he heard this the little dwarf jumped up to the ceiling in a frightful rage. He shrieked and stamped his foot so hard that he disappeared through the floor and was never seen again.

The Twelve Dancing Princesses

There once lived a King who had twelve most beautiful daughters. They slept in twelve beds all in a row and all in one room, and each night when they were in bed, the King carefully locked their door. Each night a new pair of shoes was placed under each bed and each morning, when the King returned, the shoes were quite worn through, as though they had been danced in all night and yet nobody could find out how it happened or where they had been.

Then the King made it known throughout the land that if any man could find out where the princesses went at night or where they had been dancing, that man could choose whichever daughter he liked to be his wife and he would be King after his death. But if any man tried and failed to find the secret, he should be put to death.

Soon there came along a rich prince who claimed he could discover their secret. He was royally entertained by the King, and in the evening was taken to the room next to the one where the princesses lay in their twelve beds. In this room he would wait and watch and follow them as they went out, to see what really happened. And the door of the princesses' room was left open so that he might hear all that came to pass.

But one of the princesses soon brought the prince a goblet of rich red wine which sent him into a deep sleep and when he awoke in the morning he was no wiser than before, and the soles of their shoes were again full of holes. So the King had his head cut off without mercy.

After him came many others and they all had the same luck and all lost their lives in the same manner.

Now it happened that a poor soldier, who had been wounded in battle, was passing through this country. On his way he met a little old woman who asked him where he was off to. 'I hardly know where I am going, but what I should dearly like to find out is where the princesses dance each night; then I might have a wife and in time become King.' 'I can help you there, soldier,' said the little old woman. 'Only there is one thing you must *not* do,' she said, flashing her eyes. 'You *must* not drink the wine that one of the princesses will bring to you in the evening and as soon as she leaves you, you must pretend to fall fast asleep.'

Then she gave him a cloak, saying, 'When you put this on you will become invisible, so that you can follow the princesses wherever they go without their knowing.' The soldier thanked her and said he would try his luck, and off he went to the King's palace.

He was royally entertained, as all the others had been, and in the evening he was led to the room where he was to watch. Soon the eldest princess brought him a goblet of rich red wine. But the soldier had a little bottle concealed under his chin and he pretended to drink the wine which he let trickle into the little bottle. Then he lay down, closed his eyes and began to snore very loudly as though he were fast asleep. When the princesses heard this they all laughed. 'So much for this one, too,' they said.

Then they went to their cupboards, took out all their fine clothes and dressed before the mirror. And each put on the new shoes that the King had brought them and skipped about ready to dance. But the youngest said, 'I feel rather uneasy tonight. I'm sure something strange is going to happen.' 'Silly girl,' said the eldest. 'There is nothing to be afraid of. Have you forgotten how many Kings' sons have tried and failed? As for this soldier, he was half asleep even before I gave him the wine.'

When they were all ready, the eldest went up to her own bed, and clapped her hands, and the bed sank into the floor and a trap-door flew open. The soldier watched them disappearing one after the other through the trap-door and then he jumped up,

slipped on his magic cloak and followed them. Half-way down the stairs he trod on the gown of the youngest princess and she cried out, 'Someone just caught hold of my gown!' 'You silly creature!' said the eldest, 'it was only a nail in the wall.' Down they tripped into a beautiful avenue of trees where all the leaves were silver. The soldier plucked a branch and made a loud cracking noise. The youngest princess again cried out, 'Did you hear that noise? I feel sure something's amiss.' But the eldest said, 'It is only the princes who are shouting for joy to see us coming.'

Soon they came to another avenue of trees where the leaves were all golden; then to a third, where the leaves were sparkling diamonds. The soldier broke a twig from each tree and the youngest princess shuddered with fear at each snap of the twig; but her sister told her not to be silly, it was only the princes shouting for joy again. On they went till they came to a lake, where, at the side, lay twelve little boats, with a handsome young prince in each, waiting for the princesses.

Each princess stepped into a boat and the soldier went in with the youngest. As they were rowing the prince who was in the boat said, 'Tis very odd; I am rowing as best as I can and yet, see how slowly we are moving. The boat seems so heavy today.' 'Tis the warm weather,' said the princess. 'I, too, feel very hot.'

When they reached the other side of the lake, they all landed and walked into a magnificent castle, all lit up and ringing with the sound of joyous music and the sound of drums and trumpets and cymbals.

Each prince danced with a princess and the soldier, who was all the time invisible, danced with them too. And when the princesses had a goblet of wine set before them, the soldier drank the wine of the youngest princess, who trembled with fear when she found her goblet empty before she had even put the cup to her lips.

They danced on till three o'clock in the morning, when they were forced to stop because their shoes were worn out.

The soldier slipped the golden goblet into his pocket as a token of where he had been.

The princes rowed the princesses back over the lake with the soldier again in the boat with the youngest princess, and on the opposite shore they took leave of each other, the princesses promising to come again the next night.

When they reached the stairs, the soldier hurried on in front and lay down on his bed. When the princesses passed him, they heard him snoring hard and they said, 'We are quite safe now.' Then they took off their fine clothes and put them away and pulled off their shoes and went to bed.

In the morning the soldier was ordered to appear before the King and he took with him the three twigs and the golden cup. The King asked him, 'Tell me, soldier, where do my twelve daughters dance at night?' And he replied, 'With twelve princes in a castle underground.'

And then he told the King all that had happened, showing him the twigs and the golden goblet. On hearing this the King called for his daughters and asked them whether all this was true or not, and when they saw they were found out, they indeed admitted it was all true.

Then the King asked the soldier which of them he would choose for his wife. And he chose the youngest.

And so they were married that very day amid much rejoicing.

The Giant with the Three Golden Hairs

There was once a poor man who had an only son born
to him. The child was born under a lucky star; and
those who told his fortune said that in his fourteenth
year he would marry the king's daughter. It so happened that the king of that land soon after the child's
birth passed through the village in disguise, and asked
whether there was any news. 'Yes,' said the people,
'a child has just been born, that they say is to be a
lucky one, and when he is fourteen years old, he is
fated to marry the king's daughter.' This did not
please the king; so he went to the poor child's parents
and asked them whether they would sell him their
son? 'No,' said they; but the stranger begged very
hard and offered a great deal of money, and they had
scarcely bread to eat, so at last they consented, thinking to themselves, he is a luck's child, he can come to
no harm.

The king took the child, put it into a box, and rode
away; but when he came to a deep stream, he threw
it into the current, and said to himself, 'That young
gentleman will never be my daughter's husband.' The
box, however, floated down the stream, some kind
spirit watched over it so that no water reached the
child, and at last about two miles from the king's

capital it stopped at the dam of a mill. The miller soon saw it, and took a long pole, and drew it toward the shore, and finding it heavy, thought there was gold inside; but when he opened it, he found a pretty little boy, that smiled upon him merrily. Now the miller and his wife had no children, and therefore rejoiced to see the prize, saying, 'Heaven has sent it to us'; so they treated it very kindly, and loved it.

About thirteen years passed over their heads, when the king came by accident to the mill, and asked the miller if that was his son. 'No,' said he, 'I found him when a babe in a box in the mill-dam.' 'How long ago?' asked the king. 'Some thirteen years,' replied the miller. 'He is a fine fellow,' said the king. 'Can you spare him to carry a letter to the queen? It will please

me very much, and I will give him two pieces of gold for his trouble.' 'As your Majesty pleases,' answered the miller.

Now the king had soon guessed that this was the child whom he had tried to drown; and he wrote a letter by him to the queen, saying, 'As soon as the bearer of this arrives, let him be killed and immediately buried, so that all may be over before I return.'

The young man set out with this letter, but missed his way, and came in the evening to a dark wood. Through the gloom he perceived a light at a distance, toward which he directed his course, and found that it proceeded from a little cottage. There was no one within except an old woman, who was frightened at seeing him, and said, 'Why do you come hither, and whither are you going?' 'I am going to the queen, to whom I was to have delivered a letter; but I lost my way, and shall be glad if you will give me a night's rest.' 'You are very unlucky,' said she, 'for this is a robbers' hut, and if the band returns while you are here it may be worse for you.' 'I am so tired, however,' replied he, 'that I must take my chance, for I can go no further.' So he laid the letter on the table, stretched himself out upon a bench, and fell asleep.

When the robbers came home and saw him, they asked the old woman who the strange lad was. 'I have given him shelter for charity,' said she. 'He had a letter to carry to the queen, and lost his way.' The robbers took up the letter, broke it open and read the directions which it contained to murder the bearer. Then their leader tore it up, and wrote a fresh one desiring the queen, as soon as the young man arrived, to marry him to the king's daughter. Meantime they let him sleep on till morning broke, and then showed him the right way to the queen's palace; where, as soon as she had read the letter, she had all possible preparations made for the wedding; and as the young man was very beautiful the princess took him willingly for her husband.

After a while the king returned; and when he saw the prediction fulfilled, and that this child of fortune was, notwithstanding all his cunning, married to his daughter, he inquired eagerly how this had happened and what were the orders which he had given. 'Dear husband,' said the queen, 'here is your letter, read it for yourself.' The king took it, and seeing that an exchange had been made, asked his son-in-law what he had done with the letter which he had given him to carry. 'I know nothing of it,' answered he. 'It must have been taken away in the night while I slept.' Then the king was very wroth, and said, 'No man shall have my daughter who does not descend into the wonderful cave and bring me three golden hairs from the head of the giant king who reigns there; do this and you shall have my consent.' 'I will soon manage that,' said the youth – so he took leave of his wife and set out on his journey.

At the first city that he came to, the guard of the gate stopped him, and asked what trade he followed, and what he knew. 'I know everything,' said he. 'If that be so,' replied they, 'you are just the man we want; be so good as to tell us why our fountain in the market-place is dry and will give no water; find out the cause of that and we will give you two asses loaded with gold.' 'With all my heart,' said he, 'when I come back.'

Then he journeyed on and came to another city, and there the guard also asked him what trade he followed, and what he understood. 'I know everything,' answered he. 'Then pray do us a piece of service,' said they, 'tell us why a tree which used to bear us golden apples, now does not even produce a leaf.' 'Most willingly,' answered he, 'as I come back.'

At last his way led him to the side of a great lake of water over which he must pass. The ferryman soon began to ask, as the others had done, what was his trade, and what he knew. 'Everything,' said he. 'Then,' said the other, 'pray inform me why I am bound for ever to ferry over this water, and have never been able to get my liberty; I will reward you handsomely.' 'I will tell you all about it,' said the young man, 'as I come home.'

When he had passed the water, he came to the wonderful cave, which looked terribly black and gloomy. But the wizard king was not at home, and his grandmother sat at the door in her easy chair. 'What do you seek?' said she. 'Three golden hairs from the giant's head,' answered he. 'You run a great risk,' said she, 'when he returns home; yet I will try what I can do for you.' Then she changed him into an ant, and told him to hide himself in the folds of her cloak. 'Very well,' said he, 'but I want also to know why the city fountain is dry, why the tree that bore golden apples is now leafless, and what it is that binds the ferryman to his post.' 'Those are three puzzling questions,' said the old dame, 'but lie quiet and listen to what the giant says when I pull the golden hairs.'

Presently night set in and the old gentleman returned home. As soon as he entered he began to snuff up the air, and cried, 'All is not right here: I smell man's flesh.' Then he searched all round in vain, and the old dame scolded, and said, 'Why should you turn everything topsy-turvy? I have just set all in order.' Upon this he laid his head in her lap and soon fell asleep. As soon as he began to snore, she seized one of the golden hairs and pulled it out. 'Mercy!' cried he, starting up, 'what are you about?' 'I had a dream that disturbed me,' said she, 'and in my trouble I seized your hair: I dreamt that the fountain in the market-place of the city was become dry and would give no water; what can be the cause?' 'Ah! If they could find that out, they would be glad,' said the giant. 'Under a stone in the fountain sits a toad; when they kill him, it will flow again.'

This said he fell asleep, and the old lady pulled out another hair. 'What would you be at?' cried he in a rage. 'Don't be angry,' said she, 'I did it in my sleep; I dreamt that in a great kingdom there was a beautiful tree that used to bear golden apples, and now has not even a leaf upon it; what is the reason of that?' 'Aha!' said the giant, 'they would like very well to know that secret: at the root of the tree a mouse is gnawing; if they were to kill him, the tree would bear golden apples again; if not, it will soon die. Now let me sleep in peace; if you wake me again, you shall rue it.'

Then he fell once more asleep; and when she heard him snore she pulled out the third golden hair, and the giant jumped up and threatened her sorely; but she soothed him, and said, 'It was a strange dream: methought I saw a ferryman who was fated to ply backwards and forwards over a lake, and could never be set at liberty; what is the charm that binds him?' 'A silly fool!' said the giant. 'If he were to give the rudder into the hand of any passenger, he would find himself at liberty, and the other would be obliged to take his place. Now let me sleep.'

In the morning the giant arose and went out; and the old woman gave the young man the three golden hairs, reminded him of the answers to these three questions, and sent him on his way.

He soon came to the ferryman, who knew him again, and asked for the answer which he had promised him. 'Ferry me over first,' said he, 'and then I will tell you.' When the boat arrived on the other side, he told him to give the rudder to any of his passengers, and then he might run away as soon as he pleased. The next place he came to was the city where the barren tree stood: 'Kill the mouse,' said he, 'that gnaws the root, and you will have golden apples again.' They gave him a rich present, and he journeyed on to the city where the fountain had dried up, and the guard demanded his answer to their question. So he told them how to cure the mischief, and they thanked him and gave him the two asses laden with gold.

And now at last this child of fortune reached home, and his wife rejoiced greatly to see him, and to hear how well everything had gone with him. He gave the three golden hairs to the king, who could no longer raise any objection to him, and when he saw all the treasures, cried out in a transport of joy, 'Dear son, where did you find all this gold?' 'By the side of a lake,' said the youth, 'where there is plenty more to be had.' 'Pray, tell me,' said the king, 'that I may go and get some too.' 'As much as you please,' replied the other. 'You will see the ferryman on the lake, let him carry you across, and there you will see gold as plentiful as sand upon the shore.'

Away went the greedy king; and when he came to the lake, he beckoned to the ferryman, who took him into his boat, and as soon as he was there gave the rudder into his hand, and sprang ashore, leaving the old king to ferry away as a reward for his sins.

'And is his Majesty plying there to this day?' You may be sure of that, for nobody will trouble to take the rudder out of his hands.

The Three Sillies

Once upon a time there was a farmer and his wife who had one daughter, and she was courted by a gentleman. Every evening he used to come and see her, and stop to supper at the farmhouse, and the daughter used to be sent down into the cellar to draw the beer, and she happened to look up at the ceiling while she was drawing, and she saw a mallet stuck in one of the beams. It must have been there a long, long time, but somehow or other she had never noticed it before, and she began a-thinking. And she thought it was very dangerous to have that mallet there, for she said to herself: 'Suppose him and me was to be married, and we was to have a son, and he was to grow up to be a man, and come down into the cellar to draw the beer, like as I'm doing now, and the mallet was to fall on his head and kill him, what a dreadful thing it would be!' And she put down the candle and jug, and sat herself down and began a-crying.

Well, they began to wonder upstairs how it was that she was so long drawing the beer, and her mother went down to see after her, and she found her sitting on the settle crying, and the beer running over the floor. 'Why, whatever is the matter?' said her mother. 'Oh, Mother!' says she, 'look at that horrid mallet! Suppose we was to be married, and was to have a son, and he was to grow up, and was to come down to the cellar to draw the beer, and the mallet was to fall on his head and kill him, what a dreadful thing it would be!' 'Dear, dear! What a dreadful thing it would be!' said the mother, and she sat down aside of the daughter and started a-crying too. Then after a bit the father began to wonder that they didn't come back, and he went down into the cellar to look after them himself, and there they two sat a-crying, and the beer running all over the floor. 'Whatever is the matter?' says he. 'Why,' says the mother, 'look at that horrid mallet. Just suppose, if our daughter and her sweetheart was to be married, and was to have a son, and he was to grow up, and was to come down into the cellar to draw the beer, and the mallet was to fall on his head and kill him, what a dreadful thing it would be!' 'Dear, dear, dear! So it would!' said the father, and he sat himself down aside of the other two, and started a-crying.

Now the gentleman got tired of stopping up in the kitchen by himself, and at last he went down into the cellar too, to see what they were after; and there they three sat a-crying side by side, and the beer running all over the floor. And he ran straight and turned the tap. Then he said: 'Whatever are you three doing, sitting there crying, and letting the beer run all over the floor?' 'Oh!' says the father, 'look at that horrid mallet! Suppose you and our daughter was to be married, and was to have a son, and he was to grow up, and was to come down into the cellar to draw the beer, and the mallet was to fall on his head and kill him!' And then they all started a-crying worse than

before. But the gentleman burst out a-laughing, and reached up and pulled out the mallet, and then he said: 'I've travelled many miles, and I never met three such big sillies as you three before; and now I shall start out on my travels again, and when I find three bigger sillies than you three, then I'll come back and marry your daughter.' So he wished them good-bye, and started off on his travels, and left them all crying because the girl had lost her sweetheart.

Well, he set out, and he travelled a long way, and at last he came to a woman's cottage that had some grass growing on the roof. And the woman was trying to get her cow to go up a ladder to the grass, and the poor thing durst not go. So the gentleman asked the woman what she was doing. 'Why, lookye,' she said, 'look at all that grass business. I'm going to get the cow on to the roof to eat it. She'll be quite safe, for I shall tie a string round her neck, and pass it down the chimney, and tie it to my wrist as I go about the house, so she can't fall off without my knowing it.' 'Oh, you poor silly!' said the gentleman, 'you should cut the grass and throw it down to the cow!' But the woman thought it was easier to get the cow up the ladder than to get the grass down, so she pushed her and coaxed her and got her up, and tied a string round her neck, and passed it down the chimney, and fastened it to her own wrist. And the gentleman went on his way, but he hadn't gone far when the cow tumbled off the roof, and hung by the string tied round her neck, and it strangled her. And the weight of the cow tied to her wrist pulled the woman up the chimney, and she stuck fast half-way and was smothered in the soot.

Well, that was one big silly.

And the gentleman went on and on, and he went to an inn to stop the night, and they were so full at the inn that they had to put him in a double-bedded room, and another traveller was to sleep in the other bed. The other man was a very pleasant fellow, and they got very friendly together; but in the morning, when they were both getting up, the gentleman was surprised to see the other hang his trousers on the knobs of the chest of drawers and run across the room and try to jump into them, and he tried over and over again, and couldn't manage it; and the gentleman wondered whatever he was doing it for. 'Oh dear,' he says, 'I do think trousers are the most awkwardest

44

kind of clothes that ever were. I can't think who could have invented such things. It takes me the best part of an hour to get into mine every morning, and I get so hot! How do you manage yours?' So the gentleman burst out a-laughing, and showed him how to put them on; and he was very much obliged to him, and said he never would have thought of doing it that way.

So that was another big silly.

Then the gentleman went on his travels again; and he came to a village, and outside the village there was a pond, and round the pond was a crowd of people. And they had got rakes, and brooms, and pitchforks, reaching into the pond; and the gentleman asked what was the matter. 'Why,' they say, 'matter enough! Moon's tumbled into the pond, and we can't rake her out anyhow!' So the gentleman burst out a-laughing, and told them to look up into the sky, and that it was only the shadow in the water. But they wouldn't listen to him, and abused him shamefully, and he got away as quick as he could.

So there were a whole lot of sillies bigger than those three sillies at home. So the gentleman turned back home again and married the farmer's daughter, and if they didn't live happy for ever after, that's nothing to do with you or me.

East of the Sun and West of the Moon

Once upon a time there was a poor woodcutter who had so many children, he and his wife, that he didn't know what to do. Of food they had little, and of raiment still less, but there was one good thing about them: they were all the prettiest children you ever saw, and the youngest daughter was the prettiest of all.

One evening late in the fall of the year the weather turned so cruel outside, with wind and rain and dark, that there was nothing for them to do but sit as snug as they could indoors, knitting and stitching, and watching the walls go whiff-whaff-whuff with the wind. Just then they heard something give three loud taps on the window-pane. This happened three times before the father thought he had better go out and see what was to do. When he came outside, what should he see but a big White Bear.

'Good evening, woodcutter,' said the White Bear.

'Good evening, Bear. Is there anything I can do for you?'

'As a matter of fact there is. Will you give me your youngest daughter? If you will, I can make you just as rich as you are this moment poor.'

'That will be very rich indeed,' replied the woodcutter. 'But I think I should have a word with my daughter first. Would you mind waiting?'

'Not at all,' said the Bear. So back inside went the father and explained how there was a fine White Bear waiting outside who had given his word to make them rich as rich if only he would give him his youngest daughter.

'Oh, no,' cried the daughter, 'oh no, no!' But he went on to explain just how poor he was and how hard he found it, and what a difference it would make to her brothers and sisters and how the White Bear was the politest and handsomest creature in the whole wide world, and so on, till at length she changed her mind, and having washed her face and combed her hair, and with all her rags about her, declared herself ready and went out to meet the Bear.

'Are you afraid?' he asked. 'There is no need to be. Just climb on my back with your bundle and we shan't be long.'

So on she climbed, and off they went, and when they had been some time on their way he again asked her whether she was afraid. 'There is no need to be,' he assured her. 'Just hold tight to this shaggy coat of mine and we shan't be long.'

But they rode what seemed a very long way indeed till they came to a big steep hill. There the White Bear gave a knock-knock-knock, just as you or I might knock on a door, and sure enough there was a door in the hill which opened to him, and in they went, as it were into a great castle, with walls and a roof and windows, and rooms where the candlelight sparkled on silver and gold, and other rooms which were studded with crystal and bright gems. They walked on into the castle and came to a room where there was a table laid with precious food and drink, and, 'Are you hungry?' asked the White Bear. 'There is no need to be. Just eat and drink all you want from this table and then we shan't be long.'

The next thing he did was to give her a soft silver bell. 'Whatever you want,' he said, 'you have only to ring this bell, and it will be yours on the instant.'

When she had eaten and drunk her fill, she felt so sleepy after her meal and her journey that she thought no place could be so pleasant as bed. So she rang the bell, and before it finished ringing she found herself in a lovely bedchamber, with a bed soft and white as the heart's desire, its pillows of down and its curtains silken, and all the fringes of thread of gold. There was nothing in the room that was not gold or silver, save what was satin and silk. When she had gone to bed and put out the light, someone came and lay down beside her, but who it was she did not know. In fact it was the White Bear, who threw off his beast-shape by night, when it was dark, but was up and away and a bear again before she could wake in the morning. After this fashion she lived for a while and was happy, but then there came a day when she grew silent and sad. For at home she would be talking to her father and mother, with her brothers and sisters about her, but here she was all alone; so when the White Bear asked her one day what might make her happy again, she told him how she longed to go home, if only for a month, or a week, or a day, or just one hour.

'There is no need to be sad,' said the White Bear. 'Go home by all means. Promise me one thing, though: never talk alone with your mother, but only when the rest of the family are near. For if you let her get you on your own, there is no telling what bad luck may follow.'

She promised, and next Sunday along came the White Bear and said, 'Well, shall we be off?' Once more she climbed on to his back, and held tight to his shaggy coat, and when they had travelled a long, long way they came to a fine big house where her sisters ran in and out and her brothers round and about, and where her father and mother sat at ease in the parlour, and everything was fine as only fine can be.

The White Bear said he wouldn't come in and intrude. 'But don't forget your promise.' And with that away he trundled.

At home there was such joy as defeats the telling.

For a start they just couldn't thank her enough for making them rich, and there were dresses to talk about too. Besides, they wanted to know what sort of life she was leading with the White Bear. But she was as clever as she was pretty, and the more she seemed to tell them the less they really knew. Even when her mother tried to get her alone in her bedroom, she remembered what the White Bear had told her, and for a time found excuses for not going upstairs.

But what will be, shall be, and somehow or other her mother got round her at last, till she had blabbed out the whole story, how when she had gone to bed and the light was out someone came and lay down beside her, but before morning-light he would be up and away, so that she had never a glimpse of him, and how unhappy this made her, and how all day she lived alone, and her life was dull and dreary.

'The good Lord defend us!' cried her mother. 'Why, it might be a troll you are living with. Luckily, I know a trick worth two of his. Take this piece of candle, daughter, which you can carry home in your bosom. If you want a good look at him, light it while he is still asleep, but take care, such great care, not to drop the tallow on his shirt.'

She promised, and hid the candle in her bosom, and before nightfall the White Bear came to fetch her.

'Have you been talking to your mother?' he asked. 'For if you have, we face nothing short of disaster.'

Not she, she vowed. Why should she talk to her mother? 'Why indeed?' sighed the White Bear, and his sigh struck her heart like a stone. But she said nothing to undeceive him, and soon after dark they were back in the hill.

Here, it was the old story all over again. When she had gone to bed and the light was out someone came and lay down beside her; but there was this much of change, that in the blackest minute after midnight, when she could hear how hard he slept, she rose from bed, and lighting the candle let it shine gently upon him. What she saw was a prince so young and handsome that she felt she must then and there kiss him or die. But as she bent over him to do so the candle tilted, so that three drops of tallow fell on to his shirt, and as they touched him he woke up.

'Alas,' he cried, 'what have you done? Had you been resolute for just one year I should have been freed from my enchantment. It is my step-mother who has laid a spell on me, so that I am a White Bear by day and a man by night. Now all is over between us, and I must return to where she is dwelling in a castle which stands East of the Sun and West of the Moon. A princess lives there too, whose nose is three feet long, and rosy into the bargain, and she is the one I shall have to marry now.'

'Forgive me, forgive me,' she cried to him, weeping; but there was no help for it: off he must go.

'Let me go with you, please let me go!'

There was no chance of that, he told her sadly. He must go as he came, alone.

'Tell me the way, then,' she pleaded. 'Surely I may know that, and come looking for you?'

Unhappily, he told her, there was no way thither.

The castle lay East of the Sun and West of the Moon, and that was all about it.

So she cried herself to sleep, and next morning when she woke up the Prince and the castle had gone into thin air, and she was lying on a small green mound in the middle of the forest, and all she had to wear were the rags she had worn the day she left her father the woodcutter's home. But because she was as brave as she was pretty, she stood up and determined to go looking for the castle that lay East of the Sun and West of the Moon.

She had been walking almost a day when she came to where an old crone, with three loose teeth in her head, was sitting under a high rock, playing with a golden apple. When she had greeted this crone, she asked her whether she knew the way to the Prince and his step-mother in the castle that lay East of the Sun and West of the Moon, where there lived also a Princess with a red nose three feet long whom the Prince might have to marry.

'Why do you ask?' asked the crone, and her teeth went shiggle-shiggle-shiggle. 'Are you the girl for him?'

'I would be, if I could find him again.'

'I believe you,' said the crone. 'But all I know is what you know for yourself already. But here, have the loan of my horse, who will carry you to my sister's. Maybe she can tell you more than I can. When you get there, just give the horse a flick under the right ear, and he'll come trotting home of himself. Oh, and take this golden apple with you.'

She climbed on the horse and away she went, and in time she came upon another crone, with two loose teeth in her head, sitting under another rock, carding with a golden carding-comb. Her, too, she asked whether she knew the way to her Prince and his stepmother and the long-nosed Princess in the castle that lay East of the Sun and West of the Moon.

'I doubt whether I know more than you do,' said the crone, and her teeth went shiggle. 'But here, have the loan of my horse, who will carry you to my sister's. Maybe she can tell you more than I can. Just give the horse a flick under the right ear when you get there, and he will come cantering home of himself. Oh, you had better take this golden carding-comb with you.'

Once more she climbed on the horse and away she went, and after a long and weary journey she came upon yet a third crone, with just one loose tooth in her head, spinning with a golden spinning-wheel. Again she asked much the same question, and again she had much the same answer.

'But I'll lend you this horse of mine,' promised the crone, and her one tooth went shiggle. 'Ride on and find the East Wind and ask him to help you. He has been about a good deal. And you need only give the horse a flick under the right ear when you have done with him, and he'll come galloping home of himself. Oh, and why not take this golden spinning-wheel with you?'

And now she had to ride for many days, a hard and weary time, before she reached the East Wind's home. He was in, as it happened, and told her, yes, he had heard of that place, but where it was he could not say, for he had never had breath to blow so far.

'But let us go along to my brother the West Wind. He may well have been there, for he blows much more strongly than I.'

She climbed on his back, and it is enough to say that they travelled like the East Wind and reached the West Wind's house in no time at all. The West Wind was in, as it happened, but though he had been around a good deal he had never blown as far as that castle. 'But perhaps our brother, the South Wind, is your man. He is much stronger than I, and has flapped his wings from the front to the back of beyond. He has a good memory too, and if he has seen that Three-Foot Rosy-Nosy he will be sure to remember so inflammable yet dismal a sight.'

She climbed on his back, and need we say more than that they travelled like the West Wind and reached the South Wind's house in no time at all? The South Wind, too, was at home, getting his breath back after a long blow round the southern rim of the world, but while he admitted, and admitted with pride, that he had blustered round more than most, he had never blown to the castle that lay East of the Sun and West of the Moon. 'Your only chance now is to catch our brother the North Wind. He is the oldest and strongest of us all, and the only places he has never blown on are the places that aren't there. So just you climb on my back and we'll be there in a whiffy.'

And so they were, or in two at the most. As they

drew near the North Wind's house she could hear
fluster and bluster, and the icy puffs of his breath
blew on her small, pretty face.

'Oh blow, blast, and blither!' roared the North
Wind, as they arrived at his door. 'Blow off, the pair
of you, I say.'

'Don't storm so,' said the South Wind. 'It is only I,
your brother, and the woodcutter's daughter, who
ought by rights to marry the Prince who lives in the
castle that lies East of the Sun and West of the Moon –
the one that may have to marry the Three-Foot Rosy-
Nosy instead. All we want to know is whether you have
been there and could you find the way there again.'

'Oh whiff, whaff, and whuffle!' roared the North
Wind, but more gently. 'Once upon a time I blew an
aspen-leaf there, and for weeks thereafter I couldn't
raise a puff. Still, little sweetheart, if you really want to
go there, and aren't afraid of my roaring, just climb
on my back tomorrow morning and we ought to
arrive before dark.'

All night long she heard the North Wind snoring to
draw his puff together; and then as day broke he so
blew himself up for the journey that she was afraid to
look at him. Oh, but he was big and stout and
blustery! Still, she climbed on his back when he was
ready, and then, whuff! away they went, high into the
air and far over the sea, as though no bound of the
world lay before them. Down below, what a storm
they had! Forests fell to the ground, and ships swirled
to the ocean-bottom. And all the while they drove on
farther and faster, till even the North Wind began to

get tired, and at last had hardly a fistful of breath left.
And as he grew tired the air left his feathers, so that
they drooped and drave and drifted, and the sea-
spray wetted his wings, and the crests of the waves
washed over his heels.

'Are you afraid?' asked the North Wind. And
when, trembling, she gasped out 'No' – 'That's just
as well,' he added, 'for I am!'

But they were now in sight of land, and he had just
enough blow in him to bring her ashore under the
castle that lay East of the Sun and West of the Moon.
By that time he was so weary that he lay on the sand
gasping, and it was days before he had puff enough to
blow himself home.

Next morning she sat herself down before the castle
and began to play with her golden apple. In a twinkling someone appeared and threw up the window.
You didn't have to look twice to know that this was
the Three-Foot Rosy-Nosy.

'Hey, you, creature that you are,' shouted the
Long-nose, 'what do you want for your apple?'

'Neither gold nor silver, neither price nor hire. But
if I may see the Prince who lives here, and be with
him tonight, it shall be yours.'

Well, that could be arranged, no trouble at all. So
the Princess got the gold apple, and the girl whom the
North Wind had brought was taken up to the Prince's
chamber when he was asleep. She called to him and
shook him, and all the time her tears ran like rain,
but the harder she tried to wake him the harder he
slept – and no wonder, for the Long-nose had given

him a sleep-sleepy drink. And at daylight up came the
Long-nose and drove her flying out.

Once more she sat herself down before the castle,
and began to card with her golden carding-comb. It
was the same story all over again. The Princess asked
what she wanted for it, and she made the same answer,
and that night she went to the Prince's chamber and
found him asleep. And the faster she tried to wake
him the faster he slept. And at daybreak in came the
Long-nose and drove her flying out.

So there she was the third time, sitting before the
castle and spinning with her golden spinning-wheel,
and a third time the Princess asked what she wanted
for it, and a third time she drove the same bargain,
only this time there was a difference; for a servant
who was there, and who very properly disliked the
Long-nose, who was always being cruel to her, told
the Prince that a girl had been there twice running to
see him, and had wept and prayed over him right till
daybreak. So this time, when the Long-nose brought
him the sleep-sleepy drink, though he pretended to
drain it as usual, in fact he threw it over his left
shoulder. And that, as the saying says, was that.

A third time she came to the Prince's chamber, the
girl whom the North Wind had brought, and now she
found him awake. There are no words to describe their
happiness, but at last he begged her to tell him how
she had managed to find him and the castle that lay
East of the Sun and West of the Moon.

'Nor have you come one moment too soon,' he
informed her, the minute her recital was over. 'For

57

tomorrow was to have been my wedding day with the Princess. If only we could think of a plan!' He thought, and she thought, till her head ached for him. 'I have it,' he announced at last. 'Before the wedding can take place I shall say that I want to make certain what my wife is fit for in the housekeeping line. Take washing, for instance. I'll ask her to wash the shirt which has the three drops of tallow on it. She is sure to say yes, for she has no idea who put them there. It was a Christian candle, don't forget, and no troll will get far with that. Finally, you will hear me swear that no woman shall be my bride who cannot wash those spots clean, and that is where you come in, through the window or the door, just as you prefer.'

This seemed such a good plan that they were there in joy all night. Then next morning, when the Princess had powdered her three-foot nose for the wedding, the Prince suddenly announced: 'Before I marry, I want to see what my wife is fit for in the housekeeping line. Is that fair, stepmother?

'Just look at this shirt,' continued the Prince. 'It was to have been my wedding shirt, and somehow or other it has picked up three drops of tallow. I swear, stepmother, that no woman shall be my bride who cannot wash them clean.'

The words were hardly clear of his mouth when the Three-Foot Rosy-Nosy was over the tub and into the suds, but the longer she rubbed and the harder she scrubbed, the bigger the spots became.

'What a useless thing I bred in you!' shouted the old trollop, her mother. 'Here, let me try.'

And try she did, but with no better luck, for the further she lathered and the further she slithered, the dirtier the shirt became.

Then all the rest of them rushed at the tub, and such washing and drying and sloshing and crying was never beheld before or be-since. But for all they could do, the shirt looked at last as though it had been dropped down two chimneys and pulled up three.

'I'm a lucky man I married none of you,' the Prince told them. 'But look, there's a beggar girl outside the window, and I am sure she can wash better than all you trolls put together. Come inside, girl!' he called to her, and she came.

'Can you wash this shirt clean, do you think?'

'I can try,' she said. And as she put it into the water it turned white as milk, and as she plucked it forth it grew white as snow.

'This is the girl for me, and always has been,' said the Prince, and he kissed her in sight of them all.

At this the old trollop so swelled with rage that she burst with a loud report. Then the Three-Foot Rosy-Nosy burst with a still louder one, and there were the rest of the trolls and the trollops, one after the other, bursting as though they had practised at it all their lives. And when the last report was over, and the birds were settling to the boughs, the Prince made the woodcutter's daughter his own Princess, and they carried off with them all the gold and silver, and lived happily thereafter, for three years short of three hundred, as far off as they could get from the castle that lay East of the Sun and West of the Moon.

The Emperor's New Clothes

Many years ago there lived an Emperor who was so
exceedingly fond of fine new clothes that he spent vast
sums of money on dress. To him clothes meant more
than anything else in the world. He took no interest
in his army, nor did he care to go to the theatre, or to
drive about in his state coach, unless it was to display
his new clothes. He had different robes for every single
hour of the day.

In the great city where he lived life was gay and
strangers were always coming and going. Everyone
knew about the Emperor's passion for clothes.

Now one fine day two swindlers, calling themselves
weavers, arrived. They declared that they could make
the most magnificent cloth that one could imagine;
cloth of most beautiful colours and elaborate patterns.
Not only was the material so beautiful, but the
clothes made from it had the special power of being
invisible to everyone who was stupid or not fit for his
post.

'What a splendid idea,' thought the Emperor.
'What useful clothes to have. If I had such a suit of
clothes I could know at once which of my people is
stupid or unfit for his post.'

So the Emperor gave the swindlers large sums of
money and the two weavers set up their looms in the
palace. They demanded the finest thread of the best

silk and the finest gold and they pretended to work at their looms. But they put nothing on the looms. The frames stood empty. The silk and gold thread they stuffed into their bags. So they sat pretending to weave, and continued to work at the empty loom till late into the night. Night after night they went home with their money and their bags full of the finest silk and gold thread. Day after day they pretended to work.

Now the Emperor was eager to know how much of the cloth was finished, and would have loved to see for himself. He was, however, somewhat uneasy. 'Suppose,' he thought secretly, 'suppose I am unable to see the cloth. That would mean I am either stupid or unfit for my post. That cannot be,' he thought, but all the same he decided to send for his faithful old

minister to go and see. 'He will best be able to see how the cloth looks. He is far from stupid and splendid at his work.'

So the faithful old minister went into the hall where the two weavers sat beside the empty looms pretending to work with all their might.

The Emperor's minister opened his eyes wide. 'Upon my life!' he thought. 'I see nothing at all, nothing.' But he did not say so.

The two swindlers begged him to come nearer and asked him how he liked it. 'Are not the colours exquisite, and see how intricate are the patterns,' they said. The poor old minister stared and stared. Still he could see nothing, for there *was* nothing. But he did not dare to say he saw nothing. 'Nobody must find out,' thought he. 'I must never confess that I could not see the stuff.'

'Well,' said one of the rascals. 'You do not say whether it pleases you.'

'Oh, it is beautiful – most excellent, to be sure. Such a beautiful design, such exquisite colours. I shall tell the Emperor how enchanted I am with the cloth.'

'We are very glad to hear that,' said the weavers, and they started to describe the colours and patterns in great detail. The old minister listened very carefully so that he could repeat the description to the Emperor. They also demanded more money and more gold thread, saying that they needed it to finish the cloth. But, of course, they put all they were given into their bags and pockets and kept on working at their empty looms.

Soon after this the Emperor sent another official to see how the men were getting on and to ask whether the cloth would soon be ready. Exactly the same happened with him as with the minister. He stood and stared, but as there was nothing to be seen, he could see nothing.

'Is not the material beautiful?' said the swindlers, and again they talked of the patterns and the exquisite colours. 'Stupid I certainly am not,' thought the official. 'Then I must be unfit for my post. But nobody shall know that I could not see the material.' Then he praised the material he did not see and declared that he was delighted with the colours and the marvellous patterns.

To the Emperor he said when he returned, 'The cloth the weavers are preparing is truly magnificent.'

Everybody in the city had heard of the secret cloth and was talking about the splendid material.

And now the Emperor was curious to see the costly stuff for himself while it was still upon the looms. Accompanied by a number of selected ministers, among whom were the two poor ministers who had already been before, the Emperor went to the weavers. There they sat in front of the empty looms, weaving more diligently than ever, yet without a single thread upon the looms.

'Is not the cloth magnificent?' said the two ministers. 'See here, the splendid pattern, the glorious colours.' Each pointed to the empty loom. Each thought that the other could see the material.

'What can this mean?' said the Emperor to himself.

'This is terrible. Am I so stupid? Am I not fit to be Emperor? This is disastrous,' he thought. But aloud he said, 'Oh, the cloth is perfectly wonderful. It has a splendid pattern and such charming colours.' And he nodded his approval and smiled appreciatively and stared at the empty looms. He would not, he could not, admit he saw nothing, when his two ministers had praised the material so highly. And all his men looked and looked at the empty looms. Not one of them saw anything there at all. Nevertheless, they all said, 'Oh, the cloth is magnificent.'

They advised the Emperor to have some new clothes made from this splendid material to wear in the great procession the following day.

'Magnificent.' 'Excellent.' 'Exquisite,' went from mouth to mouth and everyone was pleased. Each of the swindlers was given a decoration to wear in his button-hole and the title of 'Knight of the Loom'.

The rascals sat up all that night and worked, burning more than sixteen candles, so that everyone could see how busy they were making the suit of clothes ready for the procession. Each of them had a great big pair of scissors and they cut in the air, pretending to cut the cloth with them, and sewed with needles without any thread.

There was great excitement in the palace and the Emperor's clothes were the talk of the town. At last the weavers declared that the clothes were ready. Then the Emperor, with the most distinguished gentlemen of the court, came to the weavers. Each of the swindlers lifted up an arm as if he were holding something. 'Here are Your Majesty's trousers,' said one. 'This is Your Majesty's mantle,' said the other. 'The whole suit is as light as a spider's web. Why, you might almost feel as if you had nothing on, but that is just the beauty of it.'

'Magnificent,' cried the ministers, but they could see nothing at all. Indeed there was nothing to be seen.

'Now if Your Imperial Majesty would graciously consent to take off your clothes,' said the weavers, 'we could fit on the new ones.' So the Emperor laid aside his clothes and the swindlers pretended to help him piece by piece into the new ones they were supposed to have made.

The Emperor turned from side to side in front of the long glass as if admiring himself.

'How well they fit. How splendid Your Majesty's robes look: What gorgeous colours!' they all said.

'The canopy which is to be held over Your Majesty in the procession is waiting,' announced the Lord High Chamberlain.

'I am quite ready,' announced the Emperor, and he looked at himself again in the mirror, turning from side to side as if carefully examining his handsome attire.

The courtiers who were to carry the train felt about on the ground pretending to lift it: they walked on solemnly pretending to be carrying it. Nothing would have persuaded them to admit they could not see the clothes, for fear they would be thought stupid or unfit for their posts.

And so the Emperor set off under the high canopy, at the head of the great procession. It was a great success. All the people standing by and at the windows cheered and cried, 'Oh, how splendid are the Emperor's new clothes. What a magnificent train! How well the clothes fit!' No one dared to admit that he couldn't see anything, for who would want it to be known that he was either stupid or unfit for his post?

None of the Emperor's clothes had ever met with such success.

But among the crowds a little child suddenly gasped out, 'But he hasn't got anything on.' And the people began to whisper to one another what the child had said. 'He hasn't got anything on.' 'There's a little child saying he hasn't got anything on.' Till everyone was saying, 'But he hasn't got anything on.' The Emperor himself had the uncomfortable feeling that what they were whispering was only too true. 'But I will have to go through with the procession,' he said to himself.

So he drew himself up and walked boldly on holding his head higher than before, and the courtiers held on to the train that wasn't there at all.

Spindle, Shuttle and Needle

At the edge of a village lived an orphan girl and her godmother. They were poor and lived in a tiny cottage, where they made a modest living by spinning, weaving and sewing. The godmother was no longer young and as the years flowed on, she became too old to work. At last she was even too old to live any longer, so she called the girl to her bedside and said: 'Little treasure, I must go. I have no money to leave you, but you have our little cottage which will shield you from the wind and stormy weather. And you have also the spindle, the shuttle and the needle. These will always be your friends, and will help you to earn your bread and butter.'

After that the girl lived all alone in the cottage. She went on with her work as before and although she never became rich, she managed to keep poverty from her door.

Now it happened that at this time a charming Prince was roaming through the land in search of a bride. His father, the King, would not let him marry a poor girl, and as for the Prince himself, he did not care for rich girls. Said he: 'If I can find one who is both the poorest and the richest – that maiden shall be my Princess.'

He soon became somewhat discouraged, for this combination was hard to find. Still he didn't give up, but wandered on and on. When he reached the village in which lived our little orphan girl, he asked, as he always did, who was the richest and poorest in that place. The villagers told him the name of the richest maiden – a proud, haughty girl of high degree – and the poorest, said they, was an orphan lass who lived at the farthest edge of the village.

As soon as the rich girl heard that a charming Prince had arrived, she waited for him at her door, dressed in her Sunday best. When she saw him coming, she walked toward him with mincing steps, and dropped him a deep curtsy.

The Prince glanced at her and rode on without a word.

'She's a beauty and she may be rich,' he said to himself, 'but she's not rich and poor. No, she won't do.'

When he reached the tiny cottage at the farthest edge of the village, the little orphan lass was nowhere in sight. The Prince drew up his horse and looked in through the open window. There in the bright morning sunshine sat the girl spinning, spinning, spinning away. At last she happened to glance up from her work and when she saw the kind, handsome face at her window, she blushed a rosy red, lowered her eyes, and went on spinning as though her young life depended on it. She was so flustered she hardly knew whether the thread was running evenly or not. She was too shy to look up again, so she spun on until the Prince had

ridden away. Then she tiptoed to the window and gazed after him until the jaunty white plume in his hat was no more than a blur in the blue distance.

When she sat down to spin again, she felt strangely happy. Her heart was dancing and, without knowing it, she began to sing a little song which her good godmother had taught her long ago:

> *Spindle, spindle, dance and roam;*
> *Lead my lover to my home.*

To her surprise the spindle obeyed! It sprang out of her hand, out of the door. As the girl jumped up and looked after it in wonder, she saw it dancing merrily over the meadow, trailing a shimmery golden thread after it as it went. Then it disappeared into the blue distance; she could see it no longer.

That was the end of the spinning, so she took her shuttle and started to weave instead.

In the meantime the spindle was dancing and prancing after the unsuspecting Prince and at last it caught up with him. The Prince gazed at it in amazement.

'What do I see?' he cried. 'Can it be that the spindle wants to lead me somewhere? I will follow its thread and see what happens.'

He turned his horse around and followed the thread back.

Of course the girl knew nothing about all this. She was sitting at her work, weaving busily. She still felt gay and light at heart, she knew not why, and found herself singing the second part of the old song her good godmother had taught her:

Shuttle, shuttle, weave away;
Lead my lover back this day.

Suddenly the shuttle sprang out of her fingers and flew away, but so quickly that the girl could not see where it had gone. It darted out through the door and dropped upon the doorstep, where, all by itself, it began to weave a long narrow carpet. It was a marvellously beautiful one. On each side was a border of roses and lilies. Down the centre, on a golden ground, was a pattern of green vines with rabbits darting here and there, deer peeping wide-eyed through the leaves, and brilliant birds perching on the branches. Those birds, they looked so natural and gay, one almost expected them to sing; and everything looked as though it were growing by itself.

Back and forth leaped the shuttle, weaving wonders as it went, and all the time the carpet grew longer and longer.

The girl knew nothing of this. She thought her shuttle was lost, so she sat down and began to sew instead. She still felt strangely happy and there was a song in her heart. Without realizing it, she sang it out loud:

> *Needle, needle, sharp and fine;*
> *Tidy up this house of mine.*

At that moment the needle sprang out of her fingers and flew about the room, here and there, in and out, back and forth. It was just as though fairy fingers were at work for, before the girl's astonished eyes, things were changing like magic. Rich green covers appeared from nowhere and flung themselves over table, bench and bed; filmy curtains hung themselves airily over the windows; the chairs were suddenly soft and plushy, and a rich glowy-red rug rolled itself out over the bare floor.

The girl was so entranced she could do nothing but look on, wide-eyed and wondering. Hardly had the needle finished its final stitch, when the girl spied something through the window which made her heart thump. It was a faint white blur in the distance. It was bobbing up and down and was coming nearer and becoming clearer every minute. It was the Prince, being led by the shimmery thread to her very gate. He leaped from his horse and was now walking on the marvellous carpet – where that had come from, the girl could not tell; for the shuttle, having accomplished its masterpiece, now lay modestly beside the doorstep. When the Prince reached the door he was enchanted by what he saw. The young girl was standing there in her little plain dress, but everything about her glowed like a rose in a bush. He held out his hand to her, saying: 'At last I have found you! Yes, you are poor but you are also rich – rich in many things. Come with me, my dear, for you are to be my little Princess!'

The girl blushed a rosy red. She said not a word but she held out her little hand, and she was very happy. The Prince took her with him to his father's castle and made her his little Princess.

But her good friends, the spindle, the shuttle and the needle – what became of them? They were not left behind, but were given a place in the royal treasure chamber. Many a mortal came to see the spindle which had lured the Prince back, the shuttle which had led him to the door, and the needle which had made a palace out of a poor girl's home.

The Ugly Duckling

It was very pleasant out in the country. It was summer-time, the corn was yellow, the oats green, the hay was stacked down in the green meadows, and there the stork walked about on his long red legs and talked Egyptian. He had learnt the language from his mother. Round the fields and meadows there were large woods and within them deep lakes; indeed, it was pleasant out in the country. Full in the sunshine, an old manor house stood, surrounded by a deep moat, and from the base of the walls right down to the water great dock plants grew – so tall that a little child could stand upright under the largest of them. It was as lonely in among them as in the thickest wood; and there a Duck was sitting on her nest. She had got to hatch out her little Ducklings, but by this time she was well nigh tired out, they took so long about it, and she had very few callers. The other Ducks preferred swimming about the moat to coming up and sitting under a dockleaf to chat with her.

At last, one egg after another cracked, and said: 'Pip! Pip!' All the egg-yolks had come to life and were sticking their heads out.

'Quack, quack!' said she, and they said it too, as well as they could, and looked all round them beneath the green leaves; and their mother let them look as much as they liked, for green is good for the eyes.

'What a big place the world is,' said all the young ones; for to be sure they had a great deal more room now than when they lay in the egg.

'Do you suppose this is all the world?' said their mother. 'Why, it stretches out far beyond the other side of the garden, right into the parson's field – but I've never been there. You're all there, I suppose?' and she got up. 'No, that's not all; there lies the biggest egg still. How long will it take? I'm really almost sick of it,' and with that she sat down again.

'Well, how goes it?' asked an elderly Duck who came to call on her. 'Oh, this one egg takes a dreadful long time,' said the sitting Duck. 'It won't break. But just you look at the others! They are the sweetest Ducklings I've ever seen; they're all just like their wretch of a father, who never comes to see me.'

'Let me look at the egg that won't hatch,' said the old Duck. 'You may be sure that's a turkey's egg. I was made a fool of once that way, and I had my share of trouble and anxiety with the young ones, I can tell you, for they are afraid of the water. I couldn't get them to go in! I quacked and I pecked, but it was no good. Let me see the egg. Ah, yes, that's a turkey's egg; you just let it lie and teach the rest to swim.'

'Oh, I'll just sit on it a bit longer,' said the Duck. 'As I've sat so long, I may as well give it a little longer.' 'Just as you please,' said the old Duck, and walked off.

At last the big egg opened. 'Pip! Pip!' said the young one, scrambling out; he was very big and ugly. The Duck looked at him: 'That's a fearfully big Duckling, that is,' she said. 'None of the others look like that. I suppose it can't be a turkey poult! Well, we'll soon see; into the water he shall go, if I have to kick him out myself.'

Next day the weather was perfectly delicious: the sun shone all over the green docks, and the mother Duck and all her family came out, and down to the moat. Splash! Into the water went she. 'Quack, quack!' she said, and one Duckling after another plumped in. The water went over their heads, but they were up again in a moment and swam beautifully. Their legs worked of themselves, and now they were all out in the water, and even the ugly grey one was swimming with them. 'No, no, that's no turkey,' she said. 'Look how nicely he uses his legs, and how well he holds himself up. That's my own child! He's really

quite handsome if you look at him properly. Quack, quack! Come along with me and I'll take you out into the world and introduce you to the duck-yard, but mind and keep close to me so that nobody can tread on you, and do look out for the cat.'

So they went into the duck-yard. There was a terrible commotion there, for two families were quarrelling over an eel's head – which the cat got after all.

'Look, that's the way the world goes,' said the mother Duck – her beak watering a little, for she would have liked the eel's head for herself. 'Now then, use your legs,' she said. 'Mind and look alive, and stoop your necks to the old Duck over there, she's the most distinguished person here; she's of Spanish descent, so she's something special, and you see she's got a red rag round her leg. That is an extraordinarily splendid thing, the greatest distinction any duck can have; it means that people can't do without her, and she must be recognized by animals and men alike. Now then, look alive! Don't turn your toes in! A duckling that's properly brought up keeps its legs wide apart, like father and mother. Look here! Now then! Make a bow and say quack.'

So they did; but the other ducks round them looked at them and said, quite loud, 'Look there! Now we've got to have all this mob on the top of us, as if there weren't enough of us already; and poof! what an object that duckling is! We can't stand him'; and a duck rushed at him and bit him in the neck.

'Let him be,' said his mother, 'he isn't doing any

harm.' 'Yes, but he's too big and odd altogether,' said the Duck who had bitten him, 'so he's got to be smacked.'

'Those are pretty ducklings that mother has,' said the old Duck with the rag on her leg. 'All quite pretty except that one. He hasn't been a success; I could wish the mother would alter him.'

'That can't be done, your Grace,' said the mother Duck. 'He's not handsome, but he has a really good disposition, and swims as nicely as any of the rest, even better, I venture to say. I believe he will grow handsome, or perhaps in time he will grow even somewhat smaller; he has lain too long in the egg, and so has not acquired a proper shape.' And she picked at his neck and smoothed him down. 'Besides, he's a drake,' she went on, 'so it doesn't matter quite so much. He has, I believe, a good constitution and will win through in the end.'

'The other ducklings are charming,' said the old lady. 'Well, make yourselves at home, and if you happen to find an eel's head, you can bring it to me.'

So they made themselves at home; but the poor Duckling who had come last out of the egg and looked so ugly, was bitten and buffeted and made to look a fool by the hens and the ducks alike. 'He's too big,' they all said; and the turkey cock, who was born with spurs, and considered himself an emperor on the strength of it, blew himself up like a ship under full sail and went straight at the Duckling, gobbling and getting quite red in the head. The poor Duckling didn't know where to stay or which way to go, he was

so miserable at being ugly and the butt of the whole
duck-yard.

That was the first day, and as time went on it got
worse and worse. The wretched Duckling was chased
about by everybody, and even his mother and sisters
were nasty to him, and kept saying: 'I wish the cat
would get you, you ugly devil.' And his mother said:
'I wish you'd get right away'; and the ducks bit him
and the hens pecked him, and the maid who had to
feed the creatures kicked at him. So he ran away, and
flew over the fence. The little birds in the bushes shot
up in the air in a fright. 'That's because I'm so ugly,'
the Duckling thought, and shut his eyes, but ran on all
the same, till he got out into the wide marsh where the
wild-duck lived; and there he lay all night, for he was
very tired and very unhappy.

In the morning the wild ducks flew up and caught
sight of their new comrade. 'What sort of chap are
you?' they asked; and the Duckling turned to this
side and that and greeted them as well as he could.
'You're precious ugly,' said the wild ducks. 'But that
doesn't matter to us as long as you don't marry into
our family.' Poor wretch! He wasn't thinking much
about marrying, as long as he could be allowed to lie
among the reeds, and drink a little marsh water. There
he lay two whole days, and then came a pair of wild
geese (or rather wild ganders, for they were both he's):
they hadn't been hatched out very long, and so they
were particularly lively. 'Here, mate,' they said,
'you're so ugly we quite like you. Will you come along
and be a migrant? Close by in another marsh there's

some pretty wild geese – all young ladies that can say quack. You're so ugly you could make your fortune with them.' At that moment there was a Bang! Bang! and both the wild geese fell dead among the reeds, and the water was stained blood red. Another Bang! Bang! and whole flights of geese flew up from the reeds, and there was yet another bang! A great shoot was afoot. The sportsmen were all round the marsh, some even sitting up among the branches of trees that stretched out over the reeds. The blue smoke drifted like clouds, in among the dark stems, and hung far out over the water. The dogs went splash! splash! into the mud, and the reeds and rushes swayed hither and thither; it was terrible for the wretched Duckling, who was bending his neck to get it under his wing, when all at once, close to him, there was a fearful big dog with his tongue hanging right out of his mouth and his eyes shining horribly. He thrust his muzzle right at the Duckling and showed his sharp teeth – and then – splash! Off he went without seizing him.

'Oh, thank goodness,' sighed the Duckling; 'I'm so ugly, even the dog doesn't like to bite me!' But there he lay perfectly still while the duck shots rattled in the reeds and gun after gun banged out. It was well on in the day before all was quiet, but the unhappy bird dared not get up even then. He waited several hours yet, before he looked about him, and then he hurried away from the marsh as fast as ever he could, running over fields and meadows, and such a wind got up that he had hard work to get along. Toward evening he was near a poor little cottage, so crazy was it that it didn't know which way to tumble down, so it remained standing. The wind howled so fiercely round the Duckling that he had to sit down on his tail to keep facing it, and it grew worse and worse. Then he noticed that one hinge of the door was gone, and it hung so crooked that he could slip indoors through the crack, and so he did.

Here lived an old woman with a Cat and a Hen. The Cat, whom she called Sonny, could set up his fur and purr, and also throw out sparks, but for this he had to be stroked backwards. The Hen had very short little legs, and was consequently called 'chicky short legs'. She laid good eggs, and the woman was as fond of her as of a child of her own.

Next morning the strange Duckling was noticed at once, and the Cat began to purr, and the Hen to cluck. 'What's the matter?' said the old woman, looking all about her. But her sight wasn't good, so she took the Duckling for a fat duck that had strayed away. 'That's a splendid catch,' she said. 'Now I can have duck eggs, if only it isn't a drake! We must make sure of that.' So the Duckling was taken in on approval for three weeks, but no eggs came.

The Cat was the gentleman of the house and the Hen the lady, and they always talked of 'we and the world'; for they considered that they were half the world, and much the best half. It seemed to the Duckling that some people might think differently, but this the Hen could not tolerate.

'Can you lay eggs?' she asked. 'No! Then will you kindly hold your tongue.'

And the Cat said: 'Can you put up your fur, or purr, or give out sparks? No! Then you've no call to have an opinion when sensible people are talking.'

So the Duckling lay in a corner and was in the lowest spirits. He began to think of the fresh air and sunshine, and such a strange longing to swim in the water came on him that he could not help telling the Hen.

'What's the matter with you?' she asked. 'You've nothing to do, that's why you get these fancies; you just lay some eggs, or purr, and they'll pass off.'

'But it is so delicious to float on the water,' said the Duckling, 'so lovely to get it over your head and dive right down to the bottom.'

'Oh, yes, most delightful, of course!' said the Hen. 'Why, you're absolutely mad! Ask the Cat – he's the cleverest man I know – whether he enjoys floating on the water or diving down; I say nothing of myself. Why, ask your mistress, the old woman; there's no one in the world cleverer than her – do you suppose she wants to go swimming and getting the water over her head?'

'You don't understand me,' said the Duckling.

'Well, if we don't understand you, who is going to understand you, pray? You'll never be cleverer than the Cat and the woman, to say nothing of me. Don't give yourself airs, child, but thank your Maker for all the kindness people have done you. Don't you live in a warm room among company you can learn something from? But there! You're a rubbishy thing, and there's little entertainment in your company. You may take it from me! I mean well by you, and I'm telling you home truths, and that's how people can see their true friends. Now just do take pains to lay eggs, or learn to purr or else give sparks.'

'I think I'll go out into the wide world,' said the Duckling.

'Very well, do,' said the Hen.

So the Duckling went off and swam on the water and dived into it; but he was looked down upon by all the creatures because of his ugliness.

Autumn now came on: the leaves of the wood turned brown and yellow, the wind caught them and made them dance about, and above the sky looked cold, where the clouds hung heavy with hail and snow, and on the fence the raven perched and cried 'Caw! Caw!' for the mere cold. Indeed, it regularly gave you the shivers to think of it. The unhappy Duckling had a very hard time.

One evening, when there was a lovely sunset, a whole flock of beautiful great birds rose out of the bushes. The Duckling had never seen any so handsome. They were brilliantly white, with long supple necks. They were swans, and they uttered a strange sound and spread their splendid long wings and flew far away from the cold region to warmer lands and unfrozen lakes. They mounted so high, so high that the ugly little Duckling was strangely moved; he whirled himself round in the water like a wheel, he stretched his neck straight up into the air after them and uttered such a loud cry, so strange, that he was quite frightened at it himself. Oh, he could not forget those beautiful birds, those wonderful birds! And the moment they were out of sight he dived right down to the bottom of the water, and when he came up again he was almost beside himself. He didn't know what the birds were called or which way they were flying, but he loved them as he had never loved anything yet. He was not envious of them – how could it enter his mind to wish for such beauty for himself – he would have been happy if even the ducks had let him into their company – poor ugly creature.

The winter grew very very cold: the Duckling was obliged to swim about on the water to keep it from freezing quite over, but every night the hole he swam in became smaller and smaller. It froze so hard that the ice cracked again; the Duckling had always to be moving about to keep the water open, till at last he was tired out and sat still, and was frozen fast in the ice.

Early in the morning a labourer came that way, saw him, went on the ice and with his wooden shoe broke it up and carried the Duckling home to his wife, and there he was brought to life again. The children wanted to play with him, but he thought they meant to hurt him, and in his fright he dashed right into the milk-pan and made the milk splash out into the room. The woman screamed and threw up her hands. Then he flew into the butter-tub and after that into the meal-bin and out again. Goodness, what a sight he was! The woman screamed out and hit at him with the tongs, and the children tumbled over one another trying to catch him, laughing, calling out – by good luck the door stood open, and out he rushed into the bushes, on the new-fallen snow, and there he lay almost in a swoon.

But it would be too sad to tell of all the hardships and miseries which he had to go through in that hard winter. When the sun began once more to shine out warm and the larks to sing, he was lying among the reeds in the marsh, and it was the beautiful spring. Then all at once he lifted his wings, and they rustled more strongly than before, and bore him swiftly away; and before he knew it he was in a spacious garden where apple trees were in blossom, and sweet-smelling lilacs hung on long green boughs right down to the winding moat. Oh, it was lovely here, and fresh with spring; and straight in front of him, out of the shadows, came three beautiful white swans with rustling plumage floating lightly on the water. The Duckling recognized the splendid creatures, and a strange sorrowfulness came over him.

'I will fly to them, these royal birds, and they will peck me to death because I, who am so ugly, dare to approach them; but it doesn't matter; it's better to be killed by them than to be snapped at by the ducks and pecked at by hens and kicked by the servant who looks after the poultry-yard, and suffer all the winter.' So he flew out into the open water and swam toward the stately swans, and they saw him and hastened with swelling plumage to meet him. 'Yes, kill me,' the poor creature said, bowing his head down to the water, and waited for death. But what did he see in the clear water? He beheld his own image, but it was no longer that of a clumsy dark-grey bird, ugly and repulsive. He was a swan himself.

It doesn't matter in the least whether you are born in the duck-yard, if only you've lain in a swan's egg.

It really delighted him now to think of all the hardships and adversities he had suffered, now he could rightly discern his good fortune and all the beauty that greeted him. The great swans swam round him and caressed him with their bills. Some little children now came into the garden and threw bread and corn into the water, and the smallest of them cried: 'There's a new one!' And the others called out in delight: 'Yes, there's a new one come!' They clapped their hands and danced about and ran to their father and mother. More bread and cake was thrown into the water, and everyone said: 'The new one is the handsomest of all; how young and beautiful he is!' And the elder swans bowed before him.

At that he felt quite ill at ease, and covered his head with his wings, and knew not what to do. He was more than happy, and yet not proud, for a good heart is never puffed up. He thought how persecuted and depressed he had been, yet now he heard everyone saying he was the most beautiful of all beautiful birds. And the lilacs bowed their branches down to the water, and the sun shone warm and pleasant, and his plumage ruffled, and he raised his slender neck, and from his heart he said joyfully: 'Such happiness I never dreamed of when I was the Ugly Duckling.'

The Hare and the Hedgehog

Early one Sunday morning, when the cowslips or paigles were showing their first honey-sweet buds in the meadows and the broom was in bloom, a hedgehog came to his little door to have a look at the weather. He stood with arms akimbo, whistling a tune to himself – a tune no better and no worse than the tunes hedgehogs usually whistle to themselves on fine Sunday mornings. And as he whistled, the notion came into his head that, before turning in, and while his wife was washing and tidying up the children, he might take a little walk into the fields and see how the young nettles were getting on. For there was a tasty beetle that lived among the nettles; and no nettles – no beetles.

Off he went, following his own little private path into the fields. And as he came stepping along around a bush of blackthorn, its blossoming now over and its leaves showing green, he met a hare; and the hare by the same chance had come out early to have a look at his spring cabbages.

The hedgehog bowed and bade him a polite 'Good morning'. But the hare, who felt himself a particularly fine sleek gentleman in this Sunday sunshine, merely sneered at his greeting.

'And how comes it,' he said, that you happen to be out so early? I always supposed you were one of these night-creepers.'

'I am taking a walk, sir,' said the hedgehog.

'A walk!' sniffed the hare. 'I should have thought you would use those bandy little legs of your to far better purpose.'

This angered the hedgehog, for his legs were crooked not by choice but by nature, he couldn't bear to have bad made worse by any talk about them.

'You seem to suppose, sir,' he said, bristling all over, 'that you can do more with your legs than I can with mine. We both have four.'

'Well, perhaps,' said the hare, airily.

'See here, then,' said the hedgehog, his beady eyes fixed on the hare, 'I say you can't. Start fair, and I'd beat you in any race – nought to ninepence. Ay, every time.'

'A race, my dear Master Hedgehog!' said the hare,

laying back his whiskers. 'You must be beside yourself. It's crack-brained. It's childish. But still, what will you wager?'

'I'll lay a Golden Guinea to a Bottle of Brandy,' said the hedgehog.

'Done!' said the Hare. 'Shake hands on it, and we'll start at once.'

'Ay, but not quite so fast,' said the Hedgehog. 'I have had no breakfast yet. But if you will be here in half an hour's time, so will I.'

The hare agreed, and at once indulged in a little frisky practice along the dewy green border of the field, while the hedgehog went shuffling home.

'He thinks a mighty deal of himself,' thought the hedgehog on his way. 'But we shall see what we shall see.' When he reached home he bustled in and, casting a solemn look at his wife, said:

'My dear, I have need of you. In all haste. Leave everything and follow me at once into the fields.'

'Why, what's going on?' says she.

'Well,' said her husband, 'I have bet the hare a Golden Guinea to a Bottle of Brandy that I'll beat him in a race, and you must come and see it.'

'Heavens, husband!' Mrs Hedgehog cried. 'Are you daft? Are you gone crazy? You! Run a race with a hare! And where's the guinea coming from?'

'Hold your tongue, woman,' said the hedgehog. 'There are things simple brains cannot understand. Leave all this fussing and titivating. The children can dry themselves; and you come along at once with me.' So away they went together.

'Now,' said the hedgehog, when they had reached the ploughland beyond the field which was sprouting with young green wheat, 'listen to me, my dear. This is where the race is going to be. The hare is over there at the other end of the field. I am going to arrange that he shall start in that deep furrow, and that I shall start up there beside him in this one. But as soon as I have scrambled along a yard or two and he can't see me, I shall turn back. And what you, my dear, must do is this: when he comes out of his furrow there, you must be sitting puffing like a porpoise here. And when you see him, you will say, "Ahah! so you've come at last?" Do you follow me, my dear?'

At first Mrs Hedgehog was a little dense because she was so nervous, but she was amused at her husband's cunning, and gladly agreed at last to do what he said.

The hedgehog then went back to where he had promised to meet the hare, and he said, 'Here I am, you see; and very much the better, sir, for a good breakfast.'

'Indeed,' simpered the hare scornfully. 'How shall we run? Down or over; sideways, longways; two, three or four legs? It's all one to me.'

'Well, to be quite candid with you,' said the hedgehog, 'let me say this. I have now and then watched you taking a gambol and disporting yourself with your friends in the evening, and a very dainty and pretty runner you are. But you never keep straight. You all go round and round, and round and round, scampering now this way, now that, and chasing each other's scuts as if you were crazy. And as often as not you run uphill! But you can't run races like that. You must keep straight, you must begin in one place, go steadily on, and end in another.'

'I could have told you that,' said the hare angrily.

'Very well, then,' said the hedgehog. 'You shall keep to that furrow, and I'll keep to this.'

And the hare, being a good deal quicker on his feet than he was in his wits, agreed.

'One! Two! Three! – and AWAY!' he shouted, and off he went like a little whirlwind up the field. But the hedgehog, after scuffling along a few yards, turned back and stayed quietly where he was.

When the hare came out of his furrow at the upper end of the field, the hedgehog's wife sat panting there as if she would never be able to recover her breath, and at sight of him she sighed out, 'Ahah! sir, so you've come at last?'

The hare was shocked by her words. His ears trembled. His eyes bulged out of his head. 'You've run it? You've run it!' he cried in astonishment. For she being so exactly like her husband, he never for a moment doubted that her husband she actually was.

'Ay,' said she, 'but I began to be afraid you must have gone lame.'

'Lame!' said the hare, 'lame! But there, what's one furrow? "Every time," was what you said. We'll try again.'

Away once more he went, and he had never run faster. Yet when he came out of his furrow at the top of the field, there was the hedgehog! And the hedgehog laughed, and said: 'Ahah! So here you are again! At last!' At this the hare could hardly contain himself for rage.

'Not enough! not enough!' he said. 'Three for luck! Again, again!'

'As often as you please, my dear friend,' said the hedgehog. 'It's the long run that really counts.'

Again, and again, and yet again the hare raced up and down the long furrow of the field, and every time he reached the top, and every time he reached the bottom, there was the hedgehog, as he thought, with his mocking, 'Ahah! So here you are again! At last!'

But at length the hare could run no more. He lay panting and speechless; he was dead beat. Stretched out there, limp on the grass, his fur bedraggled, his eyes dim, his legs quaking, it looked as if he might fetch his last breath at any moment.

So Mrs Hedgehog went off to the hare's house to fetch the Bottle of Brandy; and if it had not been the best brandy, the hare might never have run again.

News of the contest spread far and wide. From that day to this, never has there been a race to compare with it. And lucky it was for the hedgehog that he had the good sense to marry a wife like himself, and not a weasel, or a wombat, or a whale!

The Grateful Beasts

There was once a man who, having lost almost all his money, resolved to set off with the little he had left, and journey out of his troubles into the wide, wide world. While it was still early in the day, he came to a village, where the young people were running about like so many half-witted hoddy-doddies, bawling and squealing with joy.

'What has gone wrong? What is the matter?' he asked.

'Matter!' says one of them; 'we have caught a mouse – a dancing mouse. Look at the little varmit! See, when we tickle her up, how she jumps and frisks about!'

But the man pitied the mouse, and said, 'Let the little creature go, and here's a handful of money to pay for her.' So he gave them the money, took the mouse, and set her free. In a trice, she had scampered off, jumped into a hole that was close by, and was soon safely out of their reach.

So the man continued on his way and came to another village. Here, on the green, he saw a host of children with an ass which, poor wretch, they were making stand up on its hind legs and jump about like a tumbler. At sight of its clumsy capers, they shouted with laughter, and thirsty and tired out though the poor beast was, they gave him not a moment's rest.

'See here,' said the man, full of pity for the ass, 'leave him alone, and I'll give you half the money left in my bundle.' So the children shared the money between them; and with a bray of delight, away trotted the ass into the cool green fields out of their reach.

Toward evening, the man came to yet another village. Here the young people had got hold of an old brown bear, which they had muzzled and taught to dance. He could hardly grunt for weariness, but they left him not a moment's peace, still pestered and persecuted him. The man gave them all the money he had left to set the beast free. Rejoiced indeed was Bruin to get down on to his four paws again; and, not waiting even to look behind him, he at once shambled off into the darkening woods.

But the man, having now given away everything

that he had in the world, hadn't even a ha'penny left
for a crust for supper. He sat down by the wayside
and began to think. The king, thought he, must have
heaps upon heaps of gold in his treasury that is of no
use to him. If I go on like this I shall die of hunger.
Surely I shall be forgiven if I borrow just the little I
need. And as soon as I have enough again, I can pay it
all back. So on he went until he came to the palace of
the king of that country.

By hook and by crook he crept his way into the
king's treasury, and took three small pieces of gold out
of one of the bags. But as he was stealing out again, the
king's guards spied him out. Refusing to listen to a
word he said, they charged him with being a thief and
took him before the judge, who ordered that he should
be shut up in a wooden chest and flung into the river.
Now, whether to make his misery last the longer, or to
give him a chance to keep alive, the lid of this chest
had been pierced with a few small holes to give him
air; and a loaf of bread and a jug of water had been
put inside it.

So there he sat, knees to chin cramped up in the
chest, bobbing sorrowfully along on the water and
drifting down to the sea. The chest had floated on not
more than a few miles when he fancied he heard
something nibbling and gnawing at its lock. Nibble-
nibble-nibble. And all of a sudden the lid sprang
open, and who, with her round bead-bright eyes,
should be sitting there but his friend the mouse.
What's more, as soon as they saw that the lid of the
chest was open, the ass and the bear, who had been

watching from the banks of the river, swam out and lugged it ashore. And rejoiced indeed was the man to be safe on dry land again.

As the four friends sat consulting together by the waterside, not knowing what to do next, there came softly swimming along with the stream a stone white as snow and of the shape of an egg.

At the sight of it, the bear cried out, 'The luck is with us, friends! This is a wonder stone, and whosoever possesses it may have everything he wishes.'

The man hastened down to the water, picked up the stone, and there and then wished for a palace, a fine garden, and a stable full of horses. No sooner said than done – there before his very eyes was a palace, a bountiful garden of trees and fountains, stables and horses all complete; and all so full of beauty that he could but gaze and marvel.

Now it came to pass after some little time that certain merchants with their servants and mules and horses passed that way. They stared in wonder, whispering one to the other. 'See now that princely palace! The last time we were here, this place was nothing but a desert. What mystery is this?'

Very curious they were to know how this had happened. So they went in through the gates of the palace, and knocked at the great door. And the man himself, out of the little barred window in the door, looked out at them.

The merchants questioned him. 'How comes it about,' they said, 'that this beautiful palace is here and this fine garden? It's a palace fit for a king; but when last we came this way, there was nought here but a wilderness.'

And the man told the merchants of the stone. They looked covertly one at another, and then again at the rare and splendid things around them.

'A stone,' they said. 'It must in sooth be a powerful and marvellous stone.'

He invited them in and showed them the stone. They asked the man if he would sell it, offering in exchange for it the whole of their rich merchandise. So rare and fine and costly was this merchandise that the man, in envy of it, clean forgot that the stone itself would bring him in an instant things a thousand times more beautiful and valuable; and he agreed to the bargain.

Scarcely, however, was the stone out of his fingers before his magical palace, his fine garden and stables, and all his possessions had vanished away; and the very next moment he found himself squatting shut up in the chest again at the waterside, his jug and loaf of bread beside him just as he had left them.

But his three friends, the mouse, the ass, and the bear, had by no means forgotten him, and came at once to his help. This time, however, the mouse, gnaw as she might with her small sharp teeth, could not loosen the lock. It stayed fast.

Then said the bear, 'My friends, there is only one thing to do; and we must do it. Let us seek for the stone again. Else all our endeavours will be in vain.' So off they went.

The merchants, in the meantime, had taken up their

abode in the magical palace. Away went the three friends, and when they approached the palace, they hid themselves in a grove of trees, and the bear said, 'Mouse, do you creep you in, peep through every keyhole, and spy out where the stone is kept. You are quick and small and secret; nobody will see you.'

The mouse did as she was told, but presently after came scampering back and said, 'Bad news, my friends. Bad news, I fear. I looked into the great chamber, and the stone dangles down from its high ceiling before a great shining looking-glass by a red silk string; and on either side of it sits an immense cat with fiery flaming eyes to watch and guard it.'

Then all three took council together again, and at last the bear said to the mouse, 'Creep once more back again, Mistress Mouse, wait till the master of the palace is in bed asleep, then nip his nose with those sharp teeth of yours, and tug smartly at his hair.'

Away went the mouse, and did just as the bear had said. This way she peeped and that way she peeped, until she came to the best bedroom in the magical palace. There, silent as a shadow, she crept up the silken hangings of the great four-poster bed in which snored the chief of the merchants, and tip-a-tapped over his huge pillow. One tug at his lanky hair, and one sharp nip of his long thin nose were enough. He woke, leapt up in his bed, clutching his nose in a fury, and shouted, 'Villainous, rascally cats that you are, and good-for-nothing; without stirring a whisker you have let the mice gnaw the very nose off my face, and the hair off my head!' He leapt out of his great bed, and drove the two cats which, with their flaming eyes, still sat in watch over the stone, out of the room.

The next night, as soon as the chief merchant was sound asleep, the mouse crept into his silent bed-chamber again, and, perched on hind legs, tail dangling, nibbled and nibbled at the red silken string at the end of which hung the magic stone, until it fell on to the thick silken carpet beneath. Little by little this way and that, she managed to trundle it out of the room and down the wide staircase until at last she came to the little round hole in the door through which she had entered the palace. Nibbling and nibbling, she made the hole large enough to push the stone through; and there stood the ass, awaiting her on the other side.

To keep it safe, he put the stone into his mouth under his long tongue; and away they went to the river. To make sure of reaching the chest in which their friend still sat grieving, the bear, who was a very good swimmer, scrambled down into the water, and bade the ass put his forefeet on his shoulders. 'Hold fast there!' says he to the ass, 'and never stir.' The mouse, meanwhile, had seated herself in the bear's right ear. And away they went.

They hadn't swum very far before the bear, lifting his mouth out of the water, began boasting. 'What think you of my swimming?' he bragged. 'Were there ever three such bold brave fellows! What say you, Master Ass?'

But the ass held his tongue, and answered never a word.

This angered the bear. 'Why don't you answer?' he growled. 'Haven't you a word in that empty old noddle of yours? Were you never taught to speak when you were spoken to?'

At this the ass could hold his peace no longer; he opened his mouth to reply and out from under his tongue and between his great teeth dropped the marvellous stone, which immediately sank and vanished.

'How could I speak?' he brayed. 'Didn't you know I had the stone in my mouth? Now it is gone for ever. And you alone are to blame.'

'Hold that silly tongue of yours, do; you do nothing but talk,' said the bear. 'Let us land, and talk over what is to be done.'

So the three of them held yet another council, and at last they went to the King of the Frogs, and asked him to call together all his subjects: their wives and children, brothers and sisters, aunts and uncles, all their relations and friends. When they were assembled together, the King of the Frogs cried, 'My people, an enemy is approaching, who is intent on devouring you one and all. But have courage; let us prepare for him. Bring in every stone large and small you can find, and a fortress shall be built to guard us against him.'

Filled with alarm at these tidings, the frogs instantly set to work, bringing up a myriad stones from out of the river and piling them up into heaps ready for the building.

And at last there came swimming along a slow, fat, bullfrog dragging behind him by the end of its silken string the magic stone which he had found sunken in the very midst of the river. When the bear saw it, he jumped for joy. He thanked the King of the Frogs for his courtesy and kindness. The King announced that all danger was now over, and his subjects were very well pleased. Besides, if any such enemy should appear, here were stones in plenty in readiness for him.

The three friends without delay set off down the river. They reached the chest in the nick of time. Every crumb of the loaf of bread had been eaten; not a drop of water remained in the jug. The good man inside the box, almost with his last breath, wished himself safe and sound in his palace again. All in a moment, as swiftly as a dream comes and goes, in his palace he was. Another wish, and the merchants found themselves, their merchandise restored, outside the palace gates once more, and unlikely to enter it again! There, in his magical palace, with its fine gardens, its orchards of fruit-trees, its birds and flowers and fountains and pleasant streams, the man and his three faithful friends dwelt together. And merry and happy were they their whole lives long.

Little One-Eye
Little Two-Eyes and
Little Three-Eyes

There was once upon a time a woman who had three daughters. The eldest was called Little One-eye, because she had only one eye in the middle of her forehead; the second was called Little Two-eyes, because she had two eyes like other people; and the youngest was Little Three-eyes, because she had three eyes, and her third eye was also in the middle of her forehead. But because Little Two-eyes did not look any different from other children, her sisters and mother would say to her, 'You, with your two eyes, are no better than common folk. You don't belong to us.' They pushed her here, threw her wretched clothes there, and gave her to eat only what they left. They were as unkind to her as ever they could be.

It happened one day that Little Two-eyes had to go out into the fields to take care of the goat, but she was still hungry because her sisters had given her so little to eat. So she sat down in the meadow and began to cry. She cried so much that two little brooks ran out of her eyes. When she looked up once, in her grief, there stood a woman beside her, who smiled and asked:

'Little Two-eyes, why are you crying?'

Little Two-eyes answered, 'Have I not reason to cry? Because I have two eyes like other people, my sisters and my mother cannot bear me. They push me out of one corner into another and give me nothing to eat except what they leave. Today they gave me so little I am still quite hungry.'

Then the wise woman said, 'Little Two-eyes, dry your eyes, I will tell you something so you need never be hungry again. Only say to your goat:

> "*Little goat, bleat,*
> *Little table, appear,*"

and a beautifully spread table will stand before you, with the most delicious food on it and you can eat as

much as you want. When you have had enough, you
have only to say:

> "*Little goat, bleat,*
> *Little table, away,*"

and then it will vanish.' Then the wise woman went
away.

But Little Two-eyes thought, 'I must try at once if
what she has told me is true. I am more hungry than
ever,' and she said:

> "*Little goat, bleat,*
> *Little table, appear,*"

and scarcely had she uttered the words, when a little
table stood before her, covered with a white cloth, on
which were arranged a plate, with a knife and fork
and a silver spoon, and the most beautiful dishes, which
were smoking hot, as if they had just come out of the
kitchen. Then Little Two-eyes said the shortest grace
she knew and ate a good dinner. When she had eaten
enough, she said, as the wise woman had told her:

> "*Little goat, bleat,*
> *Little table, away,*"

and immediately the table and all that was on it disappeared again. 'That is a splendid way to keep
house,' said Little Two-eyes, and she was quite happy
and contented.

In the evening, when she went home with her goat,
she found a little earthenware dish with the food her
sisters had left for her, but she did not touch it. The
next day she went out again with her goat and left the

few scraps given her. At first her sisters did not notice this, but in the end, they said, 'Something is the matter with Little Two-eyes. She always leaves her food now and she used to gobble up all that was given her. She must have found other means of getting food.' So Little One-eye was told to go out with Little Two-eyes when she drove the goat to pasture, to see whether anyone brought her food and drink.

Now when Little Two-eyes was setting out, Little One-eye came up to her and said, 'I will go into the field with you and see if you take good care of the goat and if you drive him properly to get grass.' But Little Two-eyes knew what Little One-eye had in her mind, and she drove the goat into the long grass, and said, 'Come, Little One-eye, we will sit down here and I will sing you something.'

Little One-eye sat down. She was tired by the long walk, to which she was not used, and by the hot day, and when Little Two-eyes went on singing:

> "*Little One-eye, are you awake?*
> *Little One-eye, are you asleep?*"

she shut her one eye and fell asleep. When Little Two-eyes saw Little One-eye was asleep, she said:

> "*Little goat, bleat,*
> *Little table, appear,*"

and sat down at her table and ate and drank as much as she wanted. Then she said again:

> "*Little goat, bleat,*
> *Little table, away,*"

and in the twinkling of an eye all had vanished.

Little Two-eyes then woke Little One-eye, and said, 'Little One-eye, you meant to watch and instead, you went to sleep. In the meantime the goat might have run far and wide. Come, we will go home.' So they went home. Little Two-eyes again left her little dish untouched. Little One-eye could not tell her mother why, and said as an excuse, 'I was so sleepy out-of-doors.'

The next day the mother said to Little Three-eyes, 'This time you shall go with Little Two-eyes and watch what she does out in the fields and whether any-one brings her food and drink.'

So Little Three-eyes went to Little Two-eyes, and said, 'I will go with you and see if you take good care of the goat and if you drive him properly to get grass.'

But Little Two-eyes knew what Little Three-eyes had in her mind. She drove the goat out into the tall grass, and said, 'We will sit down here, Little Three-eyes, and I will sing you something.' Little Three-eyes sat down; she was tired by the walk and the hot day. And Little Two-eyes sang the same little song again:

"*Little Three-eyes, are you awake?*"

but instead of singing as she should have:

"*Little Three-eyes, are you asleep?*"

she sang, without thinking:

"*Little Two-eyes, are you asleep?*"

And she went on singing:

> "*Little Three-eyes, are you awake?*
> *Little Two-eyes, are you asleep?*"

The two eyes of Little Three-eyes fell asleep, but the third, which was not spoken to in the little rhyme, did not fall asleep. Of course Little Three-eyes shut that eye also, to look as if she were asleep, but it was blinking and could see everything quite well.

When Little Two-eyes thought Little Three-eyes was sound asleep, she said her rhyme:

> "*Little goat, bleat,*
> *Little table, appear,*"

and ate and drank to her heart's content, and then made the table go away again, by saying:

> "*Little goat, bleat,*
> *Little table, away.*"

But Little Three-eyes had seen everything. Then Little Two-eyes came to her, woke her, and said, 'Well, Little Three-eyes, have you been asleep? You watch well! Come, we will go home.' When they reached home, Little Two-eyes did not eat again, and Little Three-eyes said to the mother, 'I know now why that proud thing eats nothing. When she says to the goat in the field:

> "*Little goat, bleat,*
> *Little table, appear,*"

a table stands before her, spread with food much better

107

than we have. When she has had enough, she says:

"*Little goat, bleat,
Little table, away,*"

and everything disappears again. I saw it all exactly.
She made two of my eyes go to sleep with a little
rhyme, but the one in my forehead remained awake,
luckily!'

Then the envious mother cried out, 'Will you fare
better than we do? You shall not have the chance to
do so again!' She fetched a knife and killed the goat.

When Little Two-eyes saw this, she went out full of
grief and sat down in the meadow weeping bitter tears.
Then again the wise woman stood before her, and said,
'Little Two-eyes, why are you crying?'

'Have I not reason to cry?' she answered. 'My
mother has killed the goat which, when I said the little
rhyme, spread the table so beautifully before me. Now
I must suffer hunger and want again.'

The wise woman said, 'Little Two-eyes, I will give
you a good piece of advice. Ask your sisters to give you
the heart of the dead goat. Bury it in the earth before
the house door. That will bring you good luck.'

Then she disappeared, and Little Two-eyes went
home, and said to her sisters, 'Dear sisters, do give me
something of my goat. I ask nothing better than its
heart.'

They laughed and said, 'You may have that if you
want nothing more.'

Little Two-eyes took the heart and in the evening,
when all was quiet, buried it before the house door

as the wise woman had told her. The next morning,
when they all awoke, there stood a most wonderful
tree, which had leaves of silver and fruit of gold growing on it – more lovely and gorgeous than anything
ever seen. But only Little Two-eyes knew that it had
sprung from the heart of the goat, for it was standing
just where she had buried the heart in the ground.

Then the mother said to Little One-eye, 'Climb up,
my child, and break us off some fruit from the tree.'
Little One-eye climbed up, but just when she was
going to take hold of one of the golden apples, the
bough sprang out of her hands. And this happened
every time, so she could not break off a single apple,
however hard she tried.

Then the mother said, 'Little Three-eyes, do you
climb up. With your three eyes you can see better than
Little One-eye.' So Little One-eye slid down, and
Little Three-eyes climbed up. But she was not any
more successful. Try as she might, the golden apples
bent themselves back. At last the mother grew im-
patient and climbed up herself, but she was even less
successful than Little One-eye and Little Three-eyes in
catching hold of the fruit and only grasped at the
empty air.

Then Little Two-eyes said, 'I will try just once,
perhaps I shall succeed better.'

The sisters called out, 'You with your two eyes will
no doubt succeed!'

But Little Two-eyes climbed up, and the golden
apples did not jump away from her. They behaved
properly so she could pluck them off, one after the

other, and brought a whole apronful down with her.
The mother took them from her. But instead of be-
having better to poor Little Two-eyes, as they should
have, they were jealous that only she could reach the
fruit and were still more unkind.

It happened one day, when they were all standing
together by the tree, that a young knight came riding
along. 'Be quick, Little Two-eyes,' cried the two sisters.
'Creep under this, so you shall not disgrace us.' They
put poor Little Two-eyes under an empty cask and
they pushed the golden apples which she had broken
off under with her. When the knight, who was a very
handsome young man, rode up, he wondered to see
the marvellous tree of gold and silver and said to the
two sisters:

'Whose is this beautiful tree? Whosoever will give
me a twig of it shall have whatever she wants.' Then
Little One-eye and Little Three-eyes answered that the
tree belonged to them and they would certainly break
him off a twig. They gave themselves a great deal of
trouble, but in vain. The twigs and fruit bent back
every time from their hands.

Then the knight said, 'It is very strange that the
tree should belong to you and yet you cannot break
anything from it!'

But they insisted the tree was theirs. While they were
saying this, Little Two-eyes rolled a couple of golden
apples from under the cask so that they lay at the
knight's feet. She was angry with Little One-eye and
Little Three-eyes for not speaking the truth. When the
knight saw the apples he was astonished and asked

where they came from. Little One-eye and Little Three-eyes answered that they had another sister, but she could not be seen because she had only two eyes, like ordinary people.

But the knight demanded to see her, and called out, 'Little Two-eyes, come forth.'

Then Little Two-eyes came out from under the cask quite happily. The knight was astonished at her great beauty, and said:

'Little Two-eyes, I am sure you can break me off a twig from the tree.'

'Yes,' answered Little Two-eyes, 'I can, for the tree is mine.' So she climbed up and broke off a small branch with its silver leaves and golden fruit without any trouble and gave it to the knight.

Then he said, 'Little Two-eyes, what shall I give you for this?'

'Ah,' answered Little Two-eyes, 'I suffer hunger and thirst, want and sorrow, from early morning till late in the evening. If you would take me with you and free me from this, I should be happy!'

Then the knight lifted Little Two-eyes on to his horse and took her home to his father's castle. There he gave her beautiful clothes and food and drink, and because he loved her so much he married her. And the wedding was celebrated with great joy.

When the handsome knight carried Little Two-eyes away with him, the two sisters envied her good luck at first. 'But the wonderful tree is still with us, after all,' they said. 'Although we cannot break any fruit from it, everyone will stop and look at it and will come to us and praise it. Who knows whether we may not reap a harvest from it?'

But the next morning the tree had flown and their hopes with it. When Little Two-eyes looked out of her window there it stood underneath, to her great delight. Little Two-eyes lived happily for a long time.

Once two poor women came to the castle to beg alms. Little Two-eyes looked at them and recognized both her sisters, Little One-eye and Little Three-eyes, who had become so poor they came to beg bread at her door. But Little Two-eyes bade them welcome and was so good to them they both repented from their hearts of having been so unkind to their sister.

The Three Dogs

There was once upon a time a king who had travelled
in many lands, and on one of his journeys he met a
fair lady whom he married and brought home with
him. And before long a little daughter was born to
them, and there was great rejoicing, for they were
both much loved by the people of their land. But on
the very day the child was born, a queer old dame
appeared at the palace and asked to see the king. And
when she came into his presence she warned him
never to let the child go out of doors until she was
fifteen years old, for if she did, the giants of the mountains would carry her off.

The king took heed of the words of the old dame
and gave orders that the child was to be kept indoors.

Before long a second daughter was born, and again
the old dame came and gave the same warning. Then
there came a third daughter, and everything happened as it had done before. The king and queen were
much troubled about this matter, but they gave strict
orders that the three princesses were to be kept within
the palace, and they waited with what patience they
could muster until they should be old enough to go
out. The three girls grew up to be very beautiful, but
when the eldest was within a month of her fifteenth
birthday the king had to go away to war.

While he was gone the three princesses were sitting

at their window one spring morning, looking out at the flowers in the garden, where the sun was shining brightly. They wanted so much to go out that at last they ran downstairs to the little doorway which opened into the garden. At every door a guard was

always stationed, with instructions on no account to let the princesses out, but they coaxed and pleaded until the man at this door, who did not know the reason for his orders, let them out into the garden.

For a short time they played happily among the flowers, but soon a cloud of mist came down and wrapped itself about them, then rose into the air, bearing them with it.

Messengers were sent out north, south, east and west, but they could hear nothing of the three princesses. When the king came home from the war he had to be told of the dreadful thing that had happened, and sorrowful indeed were he and his queen, alone in their great palace without their lovely daughters.

The king made it known throughout the land that anyone who brought back the princesses should have one of them for his wife, and half the kingdom for her dowry.

Whereupon many young men set off on the quest, among others, two young princes from neighbouring countries to whose ears the story had come. They started off well armed, on fine horses, for they were rich and powerful, but they were rather foolish and very conceited and set off boasting that they would soon return with the princesses and claim their reward.

In the same country, but a long way from the chief town, there lived, in a little cottage in a wood, a poor woman with her son. The son spent his time looking after three pigs, which were all they possessed. He was a good lad – brave, too, and strong. While he wandered about the forest with the pigs, he used to play sweet airs on a little wooden flute which he had made for himself.

One day, as he sat playing his pipe in the wood, there came along an old, old man with a fine big dog.

The boy thought that he would love to have such a dog for company and protection. The old man seemed to be able to read his thoughts, for he offered to give him the dog in return for one of the pigs. This the boy was more than willing to do, and the old man then told him that the dog's name was Holdfast, and that if his master told him to hold a thing fast he would do so, even if it were a great giant.

When the boy got home and told his mother what he had done she was furious, and started beating him with a stick, and would not stop for all his pleading. So then he called his dog, Holdfast, which at once rushed forward and held her fast, though without hurting her. So then she was obliged to give in.

The next day the boy went again to the forest and sat playing on his flute to the dog, which danced away to the tune in the most astonishing way. Soon the old man appeared again, accompanied by another dog, and again an exchange was made, for the boy thought it would be splendid to have two dogs to protect him. This one was called Tear, and the old man said that when told to do so he would tear even the fiercest giant to bits. The lad's mother was very naturally greatly annoyed again, but she did not beat him this time – she was too much afraid of his two big dogs!

The next day he went again to the woods as usual. Now he had only one pig left, but he had his two big dogs, which now danced together when he played on his flute.

Yet once again the old man appeared, and the third and last pig was exchanged for a third dog. This one was called Sharp-ear, because his hearing was so quick that he could hear everything which was going on for miles and miles around. He could even hear the flowers growing, so quick were his ears, the old man said.

So the boy went home quite contented with his three dogs, and though his mother was ill-pleased – and no wonder! – to find that all her pigs were gone, the boy assured her so earnestly that she should not be the loser by it, that he contrived somewhat to comfort her.

The next day he went out early hunting with his three dogs and came home in the evening heavily laden with game. The day after he told his mother that he was off to seek his fortune, and that he would be back ere long with all she could want to keep her in comfort.

He travelled a long way, and in the depths of a great forest he met once more the old man from whom he had had the dogs.

The old man asked him whither he was going, and when the boy told him he was going to seek his fortune, the old man told him to keep straight on until he came to a royal palace, and that there good fortune awaited him. So the boy kept cheerfully on his way, paying for food and lodging by playing on his flute and making his dogs dance.

At last he came to a big town, and there he saw on the walls a proclamation about the three lost princesses, for in this city was the palace of the king, their father. Remembering what the old man had told him, the boy made his way to the palace where lived the sorrowful king and queen. When he showed the chamberlain how he could make his dogs dance he was allowed to perform before their majesties in the hope that it might cheer them. And the king was so much amused at the dancing dogs that he asked the boy what reward he would like. But the boy answered that all he asked was permission to go and seek the lost princesses. The king did not think that so young a lad would have any chance of success, but he would not forbid him to go, and promised that the reward offered should not be refused if he brought back the three maidens.

So the boy set off with his three dogs, and very useful they were on the journey. Sharp-ear always told him what was happening for miles around, Holdfast carried his bundle, and he rode on Tear when he was tired, for Tear was the strongest of the three.

One day Sharp-ear ran to him and told him that they were coming to a big mountain and that he could hear one of the princesses spinning inside it. It belonged to a giant, said Sharp-ear, but the giant was not at home. When they came to the mountain Sharp-ear said that he could hear the golden shoes of the giant's horse ten miles away.

The boy told his dogs to break open the door of the mountain, and there inside sat the lovely princess spinning golden thread.

When she saw the boy she was much surprised, for she had seen no human being for seven years. She begged him to go away, for she knew the giant would kill him when he returned. But the boy would not go. When the giant returned he was furious to find the

door broken open, and cried in a voice like thunder:
'Who has dared to break open my door?'

'I have,' said the boy, 'and now I will break you.'

Thereupon he set his dogs upon the giant, and they
tore him to bits.

Then the boy took the giant's great horse, loaded it
with a sack of his treasure, and, lifting the princess on
to the saddle, went on his way. After they had travelled
for a few days, Sharp-ear came running as before and
told the boy that they were again coming to a high
mountain, and that he could hear a lady spinning
inside it. Again the giant was not at home, but this
time he was but eight miles away. Sharp-ear could
hear the golden shoes of his horse.

The dogs broke open the door of the mountain as
before, and the second princess was rescued. When the
giant arrived the dogs made short work of him, as they
had done of his brother, and the boy set the princess
on the golden-shod horse beside her sister's steed and
they set off once more.

You can imagine how delighted the princesses were
to meet after so many years. They came after some
days to a third mountain. This time the giant was but
five miles off. Inside the mountain sat the third lovely
princess weaving cloth of gold. But this time the giant
did not shout and bluster when he arrived, for he had
heard of the fate of his brothers. He put on a friendly
manner and invited the boy to stay and eat. The boy
was quite taken in and accepted the invitation, but the
princess wept secretly and the dogs seemed to be uneasy. When the meal was over the youth asked if he

could have a drink. 'Up on the hillside is a spring of sparkling wine,' said the giant, 'but I have nobody to send to fetch some for us to drink.'

'That's all right,' said the boy. 'One of my dogs will soon fetch some.' The giant was delighted, for he very much wanted to get rid of the dogs. Holdfast was given a jug and told to go for the wine. But he went unwillingly. After a time, as he did not come back, the giant suggested that another of the dogs should go to help him, for the jug was a heavy one. This time Tear was sent, but he, too, went unwillingly and had to be driven off by his master. The princess wept, but the giant rejoiced to see that his plans were going so well. Some time went by. 'I don't think much of your dogs,' said the giant, 'they are not very obedient. I expect they are chasing all over the mountain.' The boy was vexed at this and told Sharp-ear to go at once and bring back the other two and the wine. Sharp-ear also went most unwillingly, but his master insisted. But when he got to the mountain-top a high wall immediately sprang up around him, which was what had also happened to the other two. This the giant had done by the power of his magic arts.

And, now that the dogs were out of the way, the giant seized his sword from the wall and told the boy that his last moment had come. The youth was very frightened, but he kept his wits about him.

'I have but one request to make,' he said. 'Before I die I should like to say one prayer and play a hymn upon my flute.'

The giant gave his consent; but as soon as the boy

began to play on his flute the giant's magic became powerless, and the dogs, set free, came rushing down the mountain and tore the giant to pieces.

This time the boy found a golden chariot belonging to the giant, and, harnessing the horses to this, he started off to drive the princesses home.

They did not know how to thank their brave deliverer enough. He was a handsome fellow, and, as he drove along, his black curls blew out in the wind, and each of the princesses fastened a gold ring from her finger into a lock of his hair. As they drew nearer to their home they met two miserable-looking young men, and the youth stopped the chariot to inquire if he could help them. They turned out to be the two princes who had set out to seek the princesses. They had been quite unsuccessful and were now in a sorry plight, having spent all their money and wasted all their strength.

So the boy took them in the chariot, being very sorry for them. But they were cruel and treacherous, for when they heard of the boy's adventures they plotted to do away with him. The dogs were off hunting in the woods around, and the princes were able to strangle the boy before he had time to call. They threatened to kill the princesses, too, unless they swore to keep silent, and they drove swiftly away, leaving the boy lying on the path. The princesses were most unhappy, especially the youngest, for she and the boy were in love with one another, and she had promised to marry him.

But very soon the dogs came running up to seek their

master, and when they found him they licked his wounds and lay down beside him to keep him warm, so that before long he recovered and was able to go on his way. But when he came to the king's palace he found it full of gay company, feasting and rejoicing, and when he asked the cause of this he learned that that very day the two eldest princesses were to be married to the two princes, who had, of course, told lying tales about their exploits.

But the youngest princess, so he was told, would have nothing to do with the rejoicings, but sat apart and wept continually.

Then the boy asked if he might entertain the company with his dancing dogs, and when he was shown into the great hall all the guests were struck with his handsome looks and manly bearing. But the three princesses, as soon as they saw him, rushed toward him and fell into his arms. Seeing this, the two treacherous princes made a swift exit by the back door and were never heard of again.

If there had been any doubt about the youth's identity it would have been proved by the rings in his hair, but there was none to doubt his tale. And so he married the youngest princess, and in due time, I doubt not, husbands were found for the two others. But the brave lad received great honour, and when the king died was chosen to reign in his stead. The old tale says nothing about his old mother or the dogs, but I think we can be pretty sure that his mother received every possible attention and comfort. As for the dogs, I'm certain they were petted and admired by the whole court, and that when the young king and queen had a family of children, which I'm sure they had, Holdfast, Tear, and Sharp-ear guarded them, and played with them so beautifully that the royal nurses had hardly anything at all to do!

Baba Yaga and the Little Girl with the Kind Heart

Once upon a time there was a widowed old man who lived alone in a hut with his little daughter. Very merry they were together, and they used to smile at each other over a table just piled with bread and jam. Everything went well, until the old man took it into his head to marry again.

Yes, the old man became foolish in the years of his old age, and he took another wife. And so the poor little girl had a stepmother. And after that everything changed. There was no more bread and jam on the table, and no more playing bo-peep, first this side of the samovar and then that, as she sat with her father at tea. It was worse than that, for she never did sit at tea. The stepmother said that everything that went wrong was the little girl's fault. And the old man believed his new wife, and so there were no more kind words for his little daughter. Day after day the stepmother used to say that the little girl was too naughty to sit at table. And then she would throw her a crust and tell her to get out of the hut and go and eat it somewhere else.

And the poor little girl used to go away by herself

into the shed in the yard, and wet the dry crust with her tears, and eat it all alone. Ah me! she often wept for the old days, and she often wept at the thought of the days that were to come.

Mostly she wept because she was all alone, until one day she found a little friend in the shed. She was hunched up in a corner of the shed, eating her crust and crying bitterly, when she heard a little noise. It was like this: scratch – scratch. It was just that, a little grey mouse who lived in a hole.

Out he came, his little pointed nose and his long whiskers, his little round ears and his bright eyes. Out came his little humpy body and his long tail. And then he sat up on his hind legs, and curled his tail twice round himself and looked at the little girl.

The little girl, who had a kind heart, forgot all her

sorrows, and took a scrap of her crust and threw it to
the little mouse. The mouseykin nibbled and nibbled,
and there, it was gone, and he was looking for another.
She gave him another bit, and presently that was gone,
and another and another, until there was no crust left
for the little girl. Well, she didn't mind that. You see,
she was so happy seeing the little mouse nibbling and
nibbling.

When the crust was done the mouseykin looks up at
her with his little bright eyes, and 'Thank you,' he
says. 'You are a kind little girl, and I am only a
mouse, and I've eaten all your crust. But there is one
thing I can do for you, and that is tell you to take care.
The old woman in the hut (and that was the cruel
stepmother) is own sister to Baba Yaga, the bony-
legged, the witch. So if ever she sends you on a message
to your aunt, you come and tell me. For Baba Yaga
would eat you soon enough with her iron teeth if you
did not know what to do.'

'Oh, thank you,' said the little girl; and just then
she heard the stepmother calling to her to come in and
clean up the tea things, and tidy the house, and brush
out the floor, and clean everybody's boots.

So off she had to go.

When she went in she had a good look at her stepmother, and sure enough she had a long nose, and she
was as bony as a fish with all the flesh picked off, and
the little girl thought of Baba Yaga and shivered,
though she did not feel so bad when she remembered
the mouseykin out there in the shed in the yard.

The **very** next morning it happened. The old man

went off to pay a visit to some friends of his in the next village. And as soon as the old man was out of sight the wicked stepmother called the little girl.

'You are to go today to your dear little aunt in the forest,' says she, 'and ask her for a needle and thread to mend a shirt.'

'But here is a needle and thread,' says the little girl.

'Hold your tongue,' says the stepmother, and she gnashes her teeth, and they make a noise like clattering tongs. 'Hold your tongue,' she says. 'Didn't I tell you you are to go today to your dear little aunt to ask for a needle and thread to mend a shirt?'

'How shall I find her?' says the little girl, nearly ready to cry, for she knew that her aunt was Baba Yaga, the bony-legged, the witch.

The stepmother took hold of the little girl's nose and pinched it.

'That is your nose,' she says. 'Can you feel it?'

'Yes,' says the poor little girl.

'You must go along the road into the forest till you come to a fallen tree; then you must turn to your left, and then follow your nose and you will find her,' says the stepmother. 'Now, be off with you, lazy one. Here is some food for you to eat by the way.' She gave the little girl a bundle wrapped up in a towel.

The little girl wanted to go into the shed to tell the mouseykin she was going to Baba Yaga, and to ask what she should do. But she looked back, and there was the stepmother at the door watching her. So she had to go straight on.

She walked along the road through the forest till she came to the fallen tree. Then she turned to the left. Her nose was still hurting where the stepmother had pinched it, so she knew she had to go straight ahead. She was just setting out when she heard a little noise under the fallen tree.

'Scratch – scratch.'

And out jumped the little mouse, and sat up in the road in front of her.

'O mouseykin, mouseykin,' says the little girl, 'my stepmother has sent me to her sister. And that is Baba Yaga, the bony-legged, the witch, and I do not know what to do.'

'It will not be difficult,' says the little mouse, 'because of your kind heart. Take all the things you find in the road, and do with them what you like. Then you will escape from Baba Yaga, and everything will be well.'

'Are you hungry, mouseykin?' said the little girl.

'I could nibble, I think,' says the little mouse.

The little girl unfastened the towel, and there was nothing in it but stones. That was what the stepmother had given the little girl to eat by the way.

'Oh, I'm so sorry,' says the little girl. 'There's nothing for you to eat.'

'Isn't there?' said mouseykin, and as she looked at them the little girl saw the stones turn to bread and jam. The little girl sat down on the fallen tree, and the little mouse sat beside her, and they ate bread and jam until they were not hungry any more.

'Keep the towel,' says the little mouse. 'I think it

will be useful. And remember what I said about the things you find on the way. And now good-bye,' says he.

'Good-bye,' says the little girl, and runs along.

As she was running along she found a nice new handkerchief lying in the road. She picked it up and took it with her. Then she found a little bottle of oil. She picked it up and took it with her. Then she found some scraps of meat.

'Perhaps I'd better take them too,' she said; and she took them.

Then she found a gay blue ribbon, and she took that. Then she found a little loaf of good bread, and she took that too.

'I daresay somebody will like it,' she said.

And then she came to the hut of Baba Yaga, the bony-legged, the witch. There was a high fence round it with big gates. When she pushed them open they squeaked miserably, as if it hurt them to move. The little girl was sorry for them.

'How lucky,' she says, 'that I picked up the bottle of oil!' and she poured the oil into the hinges of the gates.

Inside the railing was Baba Yaga's hut, and it stood on hen's legs and walked about the yard. And in the yard there was standing Baba Yaga's servant, and she was crying bitterly because of the tasks Baba Yaga set her to do. She was crying bitterly and wiping her eyes on her petticoat.

'How lucky,' says the little girl, 'that I picked up a handkerchief!' And she gave the handkerchief to Baba

Yaga's servant, who wiped her eyes on it and smiled through her tears.

Close by the hut was a huge dog, very thin, gnawing a dry crust.

'How lucky,' says the little girl, 'that I picked up a loaf!' And she gave the loaf to the dog, and he gobbled it up and licked his lips.

The little girl went bravely up to the hut and knocked on the door.

'Come in,' says Baba Yaga.

The little girl went in, and there was Baba Yaga, the bony-legged, the witch, sitting weaving at a loom. In a corner of the hut was a thin black cat watching a mouse-hole.

'Good day to you, auntie,' says the little girl, trying not to tremble.

'Good day to you, niece,' says Baba Yaga.

'My stepmother has sent me to you to ask for a needle and thread to mend a shirt.'

'Very well,' says Baba Yaga, smiling, and showing her iron teeth. 'You sit down here at the loom, and go on with my weaving, while I go and get you the needle and thread.'

The little girl sat down at the loom and began to weave.

Baba Yaga went out and called to her servant, 'Go, make the bath hot and scrub my niece. Scrub her clean. I'll make a dainty meal of her.'

The servant came in for the jug. The little girl begged her, 'Be not too quick in making the fire, and carry the water in a sieve.' The servant smiled, but said nothing, because she was afraid of Baba Yaga. But she took a very long time about getting the bath ready.

Baba Yaga came to the window and asked:

'Are you weaving, little niece? Are you weaving, my pretty?'

'I am weaving, auntie,' says the little girl.

When Baba Yaga went away from the window, the little girl spoke to the thin black cat who was watching the mouse-hole.

'What are you doing, thin black cat?'

'Watching for a mouse,' says the thin black cat. 'I haven't had any dinner for three days.'

'How lucky,' says the little girl, 'that I picked up the scraps of meat!' And she gave them to the thin black cat. The thin black cat gobbled them up, and said to the little girl:

'Little girl, do you want to get out of this?'

'Catkin dear,' says the little girl, 'I do want to get out of this, for Baba Yaga is going to eat me with her iron teeth.'

'Well,' says the cat, 'I will help you.'

Just then Baba Yaga came to the window.

'Are you weaving, little niece?' she asked. 'Are you weaving, my pretty?'

'I am weaving, auntie,' says the little girl, working away, while the loom went clickety clack, clickety clack.

Baba Yaga went away.

Says the thin black cat to the little girl: 'You have a comb in your hair, and you have a towel. Take them and run for it while Baba Yaga is in the bath-house.

When Baba Yaga chases after you, you must listen; and when she is close to you, throw away the towel, and it will turn into a big, wide river. It will take her a little time to get over that. But when she does, you must listen; and as soon as she is close to you throw away the comb, and it will sprout up into such a forest that she will never get through it at all.'

'But she'll hear the loom stop,' says the little girl.

'I'll see to that,' says the thin black cat.

The cat took the little girl's place at the loom.

Clickety clack, clickety clack; the loom never stopped for a moment.

The little girl looked to see that Baba Yaga was in the bath-house, and then she jumped down from the little hut on hen's legs, and ran to the gates as fast as her legs could flicker.

The big dog leapt up to tear her to pieces. Just as he was going to spring on her he saw who she was.

'Why, this is the little girl who gave me the loaf,' says he. 'A good journey to you, little girl,' and he lay down again with his head between his paws.

When she came to the gates they opened quietly, quietly, without making any noise at all, because of the oil she had poured into their hinges.

Outside the gates there was a little birch tree that beat her in the eyes so that she could not go by.

'How lucky,' says the little girl, 'that I picked up the ribbon!' And she tied up the birch tree with the pretty blue ribbon. And the birch tree was so pleased with the ribbon that it stood still, admiring itself, and let the little girl go by.

How she did run!

Meanwhile the thin black cat sat at the loom. Clickety clack, clickety clack, sang the loom; but you never saw such a tangle as the tangle made by the thin black cat.

And presently Baba Yaga came to the window.

'Are you weaving, little niece?' she asked. 'Are you weaving, my pretty?'

'I am weaving, auntie,' says the thin black cat, tangling and tangling, while the loom went clickety clack, clickety clack.

'That's not the voice of my little dinner,' says Baba Yaga, and she jumped into the hut, gnashing her iron teeth; and there was no little girl, but only the thin black cat, sitting at the loom, tangling and tangling the threads.

'Grr,' says Baba Yaga, and jumps for the cat, and begins banging it about. 'Why didn't you tear the little girl's eyes out?'

'In all the years I have served you,' says the cat, 'you have only given me one little bone; but the kind little girl gave me scraps of meat.'

Baba Yaga threw the cat into a corner, and went out into the yard.

'Why didn't you squeak when she opened you?' she asked the gates.

'Why didn't you tear her to pieces?' she asked the dog.

'Why didn't you beat her in the face, and not let her go by?' she asked the birch tree.

'Why were you so long in getting the bath ready?

If you had been quicker, she never would have got away,' said Baba Yaga to the servant.

And she rushed about the yard, beating them all, and scolding at the top of her voice.

'Ah!' said the gates, 'in all the years we have served you, you never even eased us with water; but the kind little girl poured good oil into our hinges.'

'Ah!' said the dog, 'in all the years I've served you, you never threw me anything but burnt crusts; but the kind little girl gave me a good loaf.'

'Ah!' said the little birch tree, 'in all the years I've served you, you never tied me up with a gay blue ribbon.'

'Ah!' said the servant, 'in all the years I've served you, you've never given me even a rag; but the kind little girl gave me a pretty handkerchief.'

Baba Yaga gnashed at them with her iron teeth. Then she jumped into the mortar and sat down. She drove it along with the pestle, and swept up her tracks with a besom, and flew off in pursuit of the little girl.

The little girl ran and ran. She put her ear to the ground and listened. Bang, bang, bangety bang! she could hear Baba Yaga beating the mortar with the pestle. Baba Yaga was quite close. There she was, beating with the pestle and sweeping with the besom, coming along the road.

As quickly as she could, the little girl took out the towel and threw it on the ground. And the towel grew bigger and bigger, and wetter and wetter, and there was a deep, broad river between Baba Yaga and the little girl.

The little girl turned and ran on. How she ran!

Baba Yaga came flying up in the mortar. But the mortar could not float in the river with Baba Yaga inside. She drove it in, but only got wet for her trouble. Tongs and pokers tumbling down a chimney are nothing to the noise she made as she gnashed her iron teeth. She turned home, and went flying back to the little hut on hen's legs. Then she got together all her cattle and drove them to the river.

'Drink, drink!' she screamed at them; and the cattle drank up all the river to the last drop. And Baba Yaga, sitting in the mortar, drove it with the pestle, and swept up her tracks with the besom, and flew over the dry bed of the river and on in pursuit of the little girl.

The little girl put her ear to the ground and listened. Bang, bang, bangety bang! She could hear Baba Yaga beating the mortar with the pestle. Nearer and nearer came the noise, and there was Baba Yaga, beating with the pestle and sweeping with the besom, coming along the road close behind.

The little girl threw down the comb, and it grew bigger and bigger, and its teeth sprouted up into a thick forest, thicker than this forest where we live – so thick that not even Baba Yaga could force her way through. And Baba Yaga, gnashing her teeth and screaming with rage and disappointment, turned round and drove away home to her little hut on hen's legs.

The little girl ran on home. She was afraid to go in and see her stepmother, so she ran into the shed.

Scratch, scratch! Out came the little mouse.

'So you got away all right, my dear,' says the little mouse. 'Now run in. Don't be afraid. Your father is back, and you must tell him all about it.'

The little girl went into the house.

'Where have you been?' says her father, 'and why are you so out of breath?'

The stepmother turned yellow when she saw her, and her eyes glowed, and her teeth ground together until they broke.

But the little girl was not afraid, and she went to her father and climbed on his knee, and told him everything just as it had happened. And when the old man knew that the stepmother had sent his little daughter to be eaten by Baba Yaga, he was so angry that he drove her out of the hut, and ever afterward lived alone with his little girl. Much better it was for both of them.

And the little mouse came and lived in the hut, and every day it used to sit up on the table and eat crumbs, and warm its paws on the little girl's glass of tea.

The Flying Postman

Mr Musgrove was a Postman in a village called
Pagnum Moss.

Mr and Mrs Musgrove lived in a house called
Fuchsia Cottage. It was called Fuchsia Cottage because it had a fuchsia hedge round it. In the front
garden they kept a cow called Nina, and in the back
garden they grew strawberries ... nothing else but
strawberries.

Now Mr Musgrove was no ordinary Postman; for
instead of walking or trundling about on a bicycle, he
flew around in a Helicopter. And instead of pushing
in letters through letter-boxes, he tossed them into
people's windows, singing as he did so: 'Wake up!
Wake up! For morning is here!'

Thus people were able to read their letters quietly
in bed without littering them untidily over the breakfast table.

Sometimes to amuse the children, Mr Musgrove
tied a radio set to the tail of the Helicopter, and flew
about in time to the music. He had a special kind of
Helicopter that was able to loop the loop and even fly
UPSIDE DOWN!

But one day the Postmaster-General and the Postal
Authorities sent for Mr Musgrove and said, 'It is for-
bidden to do stunts in the sky. You must keep the

Helicopter only for delivering letters and parcels, and not for playing about!'

Mr Musgrove felt crestfallen.

After that Mr Musgrove put his Helicopter away when he had finished work, till one day some of the children came to him and said: 'Please do a stunt in the sky for us, Mr Musgrove!'

When he told them he would never do any more stunts, the children felt very sad and some even cried a little. Mr Musgrove could not bear to see little children sad, so he tied the radio set to the Helicopter, and jumping into the driving seat flew swiftly into the air, to a burst of loud music.

'I'll do just one trick' he said to himself, 'a new, and very special one!'

The children stopped crying and jumped gaily up and down.

He flew high, high, high up into the sky till he was almost out of sight, then he came whizzing down and swooped low, low, low over the church steeple and away again.

The children, who had scrambled on to a nearby roof-top to get a better view, cried: 'It's a lovely trick! Do it again! PLEASE do it again!'

So Mr Musgrove flew high, high, high into the sky again and came whizzing and swooping down low, low, low ... But this time he came TOO low and ... landed with a whizz! Wang! DONG! right on the church steeple.

The Postmaster-General, from his house on the hill, heard the crash and came galloping to the spot on his horse, Black Bertie. The Postal Authorities also heard the crash, and came running to the spot, on foot.

When he got to the church the Postmaster-General dismounted from Black Bertie and, waving his fist at Mr Musgrove, said sternly: 'This is a very serious offence! Come down at once!'

'I can't,' said Mr Musgrove, unhappily, '... I'm stuck!'

So the Postal Authorities got a strong ladder and climbed up the steeple and lifted Mr Musgrove and the Helicopter down.

When they got to the ground, they examined Mr Musgrove's arms and legs and saw that nothing was broken. They also noticed that the radio set was intact. But the poor Helicopter was seriously damaged; its tail was drooping, its nose was pushed up, and its whole system was badly upset.

'It will take weeks to mend!' said the Postal Authorities.

The Postmaster-General turned to Mr Musgrove and said: 'For this you will be dismissed from the Postal Service. Hand me your uniform.'

Mr Musgrove sadly handed him his peaked hat and his little jacket that had red cord round the edges.

'Mr Boodle will take your place,' said the Postmaster-General.

Mr Boodle was the Postman from the next village. He did not like the idea of delivering letters for two villages. 'Too much for one man on a bicycle,' he grumbled, but not loud enough for the Postmaster-General to hear.

Mr Musgrove went back to Fuchsia Cottage in his waistcoat.

'I've lost my job, Mrs Musgrove,' he said.

Even Nina looked sad and her ears flopped forward.

'Never mind,' said Mrs Musgrove, 'we will think of a new job for you.'

'I am not very good at doing anything except flying a Helicopter and delivering letters,' said Mr Musgrove.

So they sat down to think and think, and Nina thought too, with her own special cow-like thoughts.

After a while Mrs Musgrove had a Plan.

'We will pick the strawberries from the back garden

and with the cream from Nina's milk we will make some Pink Ice Cream and sell it to people passing by,' she cried.

'What a wonderful plan!' shouted Mr Musgrove, dancing happily round. 'You are clever, Mrs Musgrove!'

Nina looked as if she thought it was a good idea, too, and said 'Moo-oo!'

The next day Mr Musgrove went gaily into the back garden and picked a basketful of strawberries. He was careful not to eat any himself, but put them all into the basket. Mrs Musgrove milked Nina and skimmed off the cream. And together they made some lovely Pink Ice Cream. Then they put up a notice.

PINK ICE CREAM FOR SALE

Nina looked very proud.

When the children saw the notice they ran eagerly in to buy. And even a few grown-ups came, and said, 'Num, Num! What elegant Ice Cream!'

By evening they had sold out, so they turned the board round. Now it said:

PINK ICE CREAM TOMORROW

Every day they made more Pink Ice Cream and every evening they had sold out.

'We are beginning to make quite a lot of lovely money,' said Mr Musgrove.

But though they were so successful with their Pink Ice Cream, Mr Musgrove thought often wistfully of the Helicopter, and his Postman's life. One day as he

was exercising Nina in the woods near his home, he
met Mr Boodle. Mr Boodle grumbled that he had too
much work to do.

'I would rather be a bicycling postman than no
postman at all,' sighed Mr Musgrove.

Early one morning before the Musgroves had
opened their Ice Cream Stall, Nina saw the Postmaster-General riding along the road on his horse,
Black Bertie. Nina liked Black Bertie, so as they passed
she thrust her head through the fuchsia hedge and said,
'Moo-ooo.'

Black Bertie was so surprised that he shied and
reared up in the air ... and tossed the Postmaster-
General into the fuchsia hedge.

'Moo,' said Nina, in alarm, and Mr and Mrs Musgrove came running up.

Carefully they carried him into the house. They laid
him on a sofa and put smelling-salts under his nose,
and tried to make him take some strong, sweet tea,
and a little brandy.

But nothing would revive him.

They tried practically everything, including choco-
late biscuits and fizzy lemonade, but he never stirred,
till Mrs Musgrove came toward him carrying a Pink
Ice Cream.

'What's that?' he said, opening one eye. 'It smells
good.'

So they gave him one.

'It's delicious!' he cried. 'Delicious!'

They gave him another and another and another ...
He ate six!

'I have recovered now,' he said, standing up, 'thanks to your elegant ice creams, which are the best I have ever tasted!'

Then he walked outside and called Black Bertie, who had walked into the garden and was eating the grass with Nina. 'Come on, Black Bertie, we must go home,' he said, and jumped into the saddle and rode away, waving his hand graciously to the Musgroves.

That afternoon, much to the Musgroves' surprise, he reappeared again. Nina was careful not to moo through the fuchsia hedge at Black Bertie this time.

'I have reappeared,' said the Postmaster-General, 'because I am so grateful for your kindness and your ice cream that I have prepared a little surprise for you up at my house. Would you like to come and see it, Mr Musgrove?'

'Why, yes!' cried Mr Musgrove, wondering excitedly what on earth it could be.

'Jump on, then!' cried the Postmaster-General. 'I am afraid there isn't room for Mrs Musgrove too.'

At first Mr Musgrove felt a bit nervous of Black Bertie, but he was too excited to see what the Postmaster-General's surprise was really to care.

When they arrived at the Postmaster-General's house they put Black Bertie away and gave him a piece of sugar. Then the Postmaster-General led Mr Musgrove up the steps of the house into the hall, where stood a large wooden chest. He opened the chest, and drew out ... Mr Musgrove's peaked cap and little blue jacket with red cord round the edges!

He handed the uniform to Mr Musgrove. 'Please

wear this,' he said, 'and become once more the Flying Postman of Pagnum Moss!'

Mr Musgrove was very excited and thanked the Postmaster-General three times. Then the Postmaster-General took him out into the garden. 'Look!' he said, pointing at the lawn, and there stood the Helicopter all beautifully mended!

'Jump in!' cried the Postmaster-General. 'And be on duty tomorrow morning.'

Mr Musgrove raced across the lawn and leapt gleefully in. As he was flying away the Postmaster-General called: 'Will you sell me six of your beautiful Pink Ice Creams every day, and deliver them to me with the letters every morning?'

'Most certainly!' cried Mr Musgrove, leaning out of the Helicopter and saluting.

'Six Pink Ice Creams ... I'll keep them in my refrigerator. Two for my lunch, two for my tea and two for my dinner!' shouted the Postmaster-General.

Imagine Mrs Musgrove's and Nina's surprise when Mr Musgrove alighted in the front garden, fully dressed in Postman's clothes.

'I'm a Postman again!' he cried. 'Oh, happy day!'

'Moo-oo,' cried Nina, and Mrs Musgrove clapped her hands.

The next morning he set out to deliver letters and to sing his song: 'Wake up! Wake up! For morning is here!' and everyone woke up and shouted: 'Mr Musgrove, the Flying Postman, is back in the sky again! Hurrah, Hooray!'

Mr Boodle, the grumbling postman, said, 'Hurrah,

Hooray!' too, because now he would not have so much work to do. He was so excited that he took his hands off the handlebars, and then he took his feet off the pedals till the Postmaster-General passed by and, pointing at him, said, 'That is dangerous and silly.'

So he put his hands back on the handlebars and his feet back on the pedals.

Mr Musgrove never forgot to bring the Postmaster-General the six Pink Ice Creams; two for his lunch, two for his tea and two for his dinner. And every day clever Mrs Musgrove made Pink Ice Cream all by herself, till soon they had enough money to buy a little Helicopter of their own, which they called FLITTER-MOUSE. They had Flittermouse made with a hollow in the back for Nina to sit in, and on Saturdays they went to the city to shop, and on Sundays they went for a spin.

Often Mr Musgrove did musical sky stunts in Flittermouse for the children, but he was careful never to fly low over the church steeple.

The Fantastic Tale of the Plucky Sailor and the Postage Stamp

A mighty liner was just about to leave Cape Town harbour for England when a frail, agitated little old lady came puffing breathlessly up the gangway. A small, stout sailor who was whistling gaily as he bustled about on deck asked if he could be of any help. She began telling him a long story all about her dear son, and would have gone on for ages had not our sailor brought her politely to the point and asked her exactly what she wanted. She looked a bit hurt and asked if he could possibly post a letter for her dear boy who was in England. 'Certainly,' said the little seaman, whereupon the old lady walked off down the gangway and the liner began to move slowly from the harbour out into the open sea.

The sailor's name was Sebastian, and being a very efficient little mariner he went straight to give the letter to the ship's postman. (I don't know whether liners have postmen on board but this particular one did anyway.) Sebastian was just holding out the letter to hand to the postman when the captain, who was taking a bit of fresh air on deck, happened to notice that it bore no postage stamp. 'Look here,' he called out gruffly, 'I'm not fussy, but you know the regulations – no stamp, no letter.' Was our Sebastian daunted? No, not he! He walked all round the boat asking everyone he came across if they had a stamp, until finally he found someone. The 'someone' happened to be extremely drunk, smelling strongly of beer. He was leaning unsteadily over the ship's side and was just handing over the stamp when Sebastian, over-eager to get hold of it, dropped it and down it fluttered into the foaming, blue breakers. But was our little sailor daunted? No, not he! He jumped head first into the sea and began swimming vigorously after it. He had just caught up with it when a great, goggle-eyed shark poked his clumsy head out of the water and gobbled it up. Was our stout Sebastian daunted? No, not he! He took out his jack-knife and with a mighty thrust slit the monster in two.

Unfortunately, just at the point where he had sliced the shark, his knife had also divided the stamp into two clean halves. Swiftly Sebastian shot out his arm to grab them, caught one and saw the other speed off on the crest of a wave. Pocketing the one half, he darted in hot pursuit after the other. With a few deft strokes he was very soon within reach and very carefully put out his thumb and two fingers to seize the elusive morsel of curly stamp. At that critical split second, out sprang a dolphin and carelessly swallowed it up. 'Things are obviously against me today,' thought Sebastian, but with lightning presence of mind he again whipped out his trusty jack-knife and with a powerful downward stroke sundered that impertinent fish in two. To his surprise, he saw two small portions of stamp, of equal size, emerging from the fish's entrails! Again his expert knifemanship had cut the half-stamp into two exact quarters!

Disappointed, but not daunted, he tried to scoop the two minute pieces into his hand. This time he found himself competing with a minnow who, mistaking the coloured scraps of paper for some dainty titbits, delicately swallowed one of them up just as Sebastian seized the other and stuffed it into his waterproof pocket. But did he bring his jack-knife into operation to extract the missing portion from the darling little minnow? Oh no! Sebastian was far too tenderhearted! His hand went groping after the slippery creature and soon it lay wriggling but secure in his palm. Then gently tickling its throat with his little finger, he coaxed the reluctant fish to splutter

out the paper fragment which again found its way into Sebastian's pocket. The minnow darted off, somewhat dazed, and our stout little sailor, realizing after a lightning check-up that he was now in possession of the complete stamp, turned and headed back to the ship.

Swimming powerfully and confidently, and shooting swiftly past any dangerous-looking sea-monsters, he was soon quite close to the liner, where he could see a large throng of passengers waving and cheering over the ship's rail. Panting slightly, he climbed the rope-ladder and was welcomed back on board amid great cheers and applause. Pressed to relate his adventures, he modestly recounted a few details to his astounded audience. The ship's postman was very impressed and went to call the captain, who had been standing a little way off, very aloof, and apparently unaware of what had happened. At the postman's request, Sebastian briefly repeated his tale. 'I should be more impressed,' said the skipper when our sailor had finished, 'if he could give some proof that what he has related is really true.' Whereupon Sebastian carefully took out the parts of the stamp from his pocket – one half and two quarters – and exposed them respectfully to his captain's gaze. 'That's all very well,' said the latter, trying to change the subject, 'but how are you going to stick the stamps on without any glue? You know my motto, "No glue, no stamp, and no stamp, no letter".' With that he turned on his heel and walked abruptly away.

But was our little sailor daunted? No, not he!

Taking a deep, deep breath he walked to the ship's side and dived into the sea before the startled gaze of the assembled onlookers. Not pausing to think that he might easily have found some glue on board ship, our stout-hearted mariner, on the impulse of the moment, had decided to swim back to Cape Town. And swim he did, without pause, until he arrived at the beach and lay down on the hot yellow sands quite exhausted. After a short snooze, he got up refreshed, stretched his legs and arms and began to notice that there were very few people about and that the shops were closed. He stopped a passer-by and discovered to his great disappointment that it was early closing day. He was just about to fling his arms up in despair when his eyes lighted on an automatic stamp-machine. 'What a confounded idiot I've been,' grunted the sailor softly to himself, 'looking for a glue shop when all I need is a stamp!' He bought the stamp from the machine and once he had stuck it on it seemed perfectly natural to put it in the letter-box.

Now why the old lady had not done this in the first place will for ever remain a mystery. However, the letter was now safely posted and Sebastian quickly made his way back to the beach and started his long swim back to the ship. And what a tremendous crowd awaited him on deck! Every single passenger and every man-jack in the crew was there and the captain personally helped him on to the deck. The voyage to England was the happiest he had ever made and he was treated like a royal personage the whole way.

The Elephant's Child

In the High and Far-Off Times the Elephant, O Best
Beloved, had no trunk. He had only a blackish,
bulgy nose, as big as a boot, that he could wriggle
about from side to side; but he couldn't pick up things
with it. But there was one Elephant – a new Elephant
– an Elephant's Child – who was full of 'satiable
curtiosity, and that means he asked ever so many
questions. And he lived in Africa, and he filled all
Africa with his 'satiable curtiosities. He asked his tall
aunt, the Ostrich, why her tail-feathers grew just so,
and his tall aunt the Ostrich, spanked him with her
hard, hard claw. He asked his tall uncle, the Giraffe,
what made his skin spotty, and his tall uncle, the
Giraffe, spanked him with his hard, hard hoof. And
still he was full of 'satiable curtiosity! He asked his
broad aunt, the Hippopotamus, why her eyes were red,
and his broad aunt, the Hippopotamus, spanked him
with her broad, broad hoof; and he asked his hairy
uncle, the Baboon, why melons tasted just so, and his
hairy uncle, the Baboon, spanked him with his hairy,
hairy paw. And still he was full of 'satiable curtiosity!
He asked questions about everything that he saw, or
heard, or felt, or smelt, or touched, and all his uncles
and aunts spanked him. And still he was full of
'satiable curtiosity!

One fine morning in the middle of the Precession of

the Equinoxes this 'satiable Elephant's Child asked a new fine question that he had never asked before. He asked, 'What does the Crocodile have for dinner?' Then everybody said, 'Hush!' in a loud and dretful tone, and they spanked him immediately and directly, without stopping, for a long time.

By and by, when that was finished, he came upon Kolokolo Bird sitting in the middle of a wait-a-bit thorn-bush, and he said, 'My father has spanked me, and my mother has spanked me; all my aunts and uncles have spanked me for my 'satiable curtiosity; and still I want to know what the Crocodile has for dinner!'

Then the Kolokolo Bird said with a mournful cry, 'Go to the banks of the great, grey-green, greasy

Limpopo River, all set about with fever-trees, and find out.'

That very next morning, when there was nothing left of the Equinoxes, because the Precession had preceded according to precedent, this 'satiable Elephant's Child took a hundred pounds of bananas (the little short red kind), and a hundred pounds of sugar-cane (the long purple kind), and seventeen melons (the greeny-crackly kind), and said to all his dear families, 'Good-bye. I am going to the great, grey-green, greasy Limpopo River, all set about with fever-trees, to find out what the Crocodile has for dinner.' And they all spanked him once more for luck, though he asked them most politely to stop.

Then he went away, a little warm, but not at all astonished, eating melons, and throwing the rind about, because he could not pick it up.

He went from Graham's Town to Kimberley, and from Kimberley to Khama's Country, and from Khama's Country he went east by north, eating melons all the time, till at last he came to the banks of the great, grey-green, greasy Limpopo River, all set about with fever-trees, precisely as Kolokolo Bird had said.

Now you must know and understand, O Best Beloved, that till that very week, and day, and hour, and minute, this 'satiable Elephant's Child had never seen a Crocodile, and did not know what one was like. It was all his 'satiable curtiosity.

The first thing he found was a Bi-Coloured-Python-Rock-Snake curled round a rock.

' 'Scuse me,' said the Elephant's Child most politely, 'but have you seen such a thing as a Crocodile in these promiscuous parts?'

'Have I seen a Crocodile?' said the Bi-Coloured-Python-Rock-Snake, in a voice of dretful scorn. 'What will you ask me next?'

' 'Scuse me,' said the Elephant's Child, 'but could you kindly tell me what he has for dinner?'

Then the Bi-Coloured-Python-Rock-Snake uncoiled himself very quickly from the rock, and spanked the Elephant's Child with his scalesome, flailsome tail.

'That is odd,' said the Elephant's Child, 'because my father and my mother, and my uncle and my aunt, not to mention my other aunt, the Hippopotamus, and my other uncle, the Baboon, have all spanked me for my 'satiable curtiosity – and I suppose this is the same thing.'

So he said good-bye very politely to the Bi-Coloured-Python-Rock-Snake, and helped to coil him up on the rock again, and went on, a little warm, but not at all astonished, eating melons, and throwing the rind about, because he could not pick it up, till he trod on what he thought was a log of wood at the very edge of the great, grey-green, greasy Limpopo River, all set about with fever-trees.

But it was really the Crocodile, O Best Beloved, and the Crocodile winked one eye – like this!

' 'Scuse me,' said the Elephant's Child most politely, 'but do you happen to have seen a Crocodile in these promiscuous parts?'

Then the Crocodile winked the other eye, and lifted
half his tail out of the mud; and the Elephant's Child
stepped back most politely, because he did not wish to
be spanked again. 'Come hither, Little One,' said the
Crocodile. 'Why do you ask such things?'

' 'Scuse me,' said the Elephant's Child most politely,
'but my father has spanked me, my mother has
spanked me, not to mention my tall aunt, the Ostrich,
and my tall uncle, the Giraffe, who can kick ever so
hard, as well as my broad aunt, the Hippopotamus,
and my hairy uncle, the Baboon, and including the
Bi-Coloured-Python-Rock-Snake, with the scalesome,
flailsome tail, just up the bank, who spanks harder
than any of them; and so, if it's quite all the same to
you, I don't want to be spanked any more.'

'Come hither, Little One,' said the Crocodile, 'for
I am the Crocodile,' and he wept crocodile-tears to
show it was quite true.

Then the Elephant's Child grew all breathless, and
panted, and kneeled down on the bank and said, 'You
are the very person I have been looking for all these
long days. Will you please tell me what you have for
dinner?'

'Come hither, Little One,' said the Crocodile, 'and
I'll whisper.'

Then the Elephant's Child put his head down close
to the Crocodile's musky, tusky mouth, and the
Crocodile caught him by his little nose, which up to
that very week, day, hour, and minute, had been no
bigger than a boot, though much more useful.

'I think,' said the Crocodile – and he said it between his teeth, like this – 'I think today I will begin with Elephant's Child!'

At this, O Best Beloved, the Elephant's Child was much annoyed, and he said, speaking through his nose, like this, 'Led go! You are hurtig be!'

Then the Bi-Coloured-Python-Rock-Snake scuffed down from the bank and said, 'My young friend, if you do not now, immediately and instantly, pull as hard as ever you can, it is my opinion that your acquaintance in the large-pattern leather ulster' (and by this he meant the Crocodile) 'will jerk you into yonder limpid stream before you can say Jack Robinson.'

This is the way Bi-Coloured-Python-Rock-Snakes always talk.

Then the Elephant's Child sat back on his little haunches, and pulled, and pulled, and pulled, and his nose began to stretch. And the Crocodile floundered into the water, making it all creamy with great sweeps of his tail, and he pulled, and pulled, and pulled.

And the Elephant's Child's nose kept on stretching; and the Elephant's Child spread all his little four legs and pulled, and pulled, and pulled, and his nose kept on stretching; and the Crocodile threshed his tail like an oar, and he pulled, and pulled, and pulled, and at each pull the Elephant's Child's nose grew longer and longer – and it hurt him hijjus!

Then the Elephant's Child felt his legs slipping, and he said through his nose, which was now nearly five feet long, 'This is too butch for be!'

Then the Bi-Coloured-Python-Rock-Snake came down from the bank, and knotted himself in a double-clove-hitch round the Elephant's Child's hind-legs, and said, 'Rash and inexperienced traveller, we will now seriously devote ourselves to a little high tension, because if we do not, it is my impression that yonder self-propelling man-of-war with the armour-plated upper deck' (and by this, O Best Beloved, he meant the Crocodile) 'will permanently vitiate your future career.'

That is the way all Bi-Coloured-Python-Rock-Snakes always talk.

So he pulled, and the Elephant's Child pulled, and the Crocodile pulled; but the Elephant's Child and the Bi-Coloured-Python-Rock-Snake pulled hardest; and at last the Crocodile let go of the Elephant's Child's nose with a plop that you could hear all up and down the Limpopo.

Then the Elephant's Child sat down most hard and sudden; but first he was careful to say 'Thank you' to the Bi-Coloured-Python-Rock-Snake; and next he was kind to his poor pulled nose, and wrapped it all up in cool banana leaves, and hung it in the great, grey-green, greasy Limpopo to cool.

'What are you doing that for?' said the Bi-Coloured-Python-Rock-Snake.

' 'Scuse me,' said the Elephant's Child, 'but my nose is badly out of shape, and I am waiting for it to shrink.'

'Then you will have to wait a long time,' said the Bi-Coloured-Python-Rock-Snake. 'Some people do not know what is good for them.'

The Elephant's Child sat there for three days waiting for his nose to shrink. But it never grew any shorter, and, besides, it made him squint. For, O Best Beloved, you will see and understand that the Crocodile had pulled it out into a really truly trunk same as all Elephants have today.

At the end of the third day a fly came and stung him on the shoulder, and before he knew what he was doing he lifted up his trunk and hit that fly dead with the end of it.

'Vantage number one!' said the Bi-Coloured-Python-Rock-Snake. 'You couldn't have done that with a mere-smear nose. Try and eat a little now.'

Before he thought what he was doing the Elephant's Child put out his trunk and plucked a large bundle of grass, dusted it clean against his fore-legs, and stuffed it into his own mouth.

'Vantage number two!' said the Bi-Coloured-Python-Rock-Snake. 'You couldn't have done that with a mere-smear nose. Don't you think the sun is very hot here?'

'It is,' said the Elephant's Child, and before he thought what he was doing he schlooped up a schloop of mud from the banks of the great, grey-green, greasy Limpopo, and slapped it on his head, where it made a cool schloopy-sloshy mud-cap all trickly behind his ears.

'Vantage number three!' said the Bi-Coloured-Python-Rock-Snake. 'You couldn't have done that with a mere-smear nose. Now how do you feel about being spanked again?'

' 'Scuse me,' said the Elephant's Child, 'but I should not like it at all.'

'How would you like to spank somebody?' said the Bi-Coloured-Python-Rock-Snake.

'I should like it very much indeed,' said the Elephant's Child.

'Well,' said the Bi-Coloured-Python-Rock-Snake, 'you will find that new nose of yours very useful to spank people with.'

'Thank you,' said the Elephant's Child, 'I'll remember that; and now I think I'll go home to all my dear families and try.'

So the Elephant's Child went home across Africa frisking and whisking his trunk. When he wanted fruit to eat he pulled fruit down from a tree, instead of waiting for it to fall as he used to do. When he wanted grass he plucked grass up from the ground, instead of going on his knees as he used to do. When the flies bit him he broke off the branch of a tree and used it as a fly-whisk; and he made himself a new, cool, slushy-squshy mud-cap whenever the sun was hot. When he felt lonely walking through Africa he sang to himself down his trunk, and the noise was louder than several brass bands. He went specially out of his way to find a broad Hippopotamus (she was no relation of his), and he spanked her very hard, to make sure that the Bi-Coloured-Python-Rock-Snake had spoken the truth about his new trunk. The rest of the time he picked up the melon-rinds that he had dropped on his way to the Limpopo – for he was a Tidy Pachyderm.

One dark evening he came back to all his dear

families, and he coiled up his trunk and said, 'How do you do?' They were very glad to see him, and immediately said, 'Come here and be spanked for your 'satiable curtiosity.'

'Pooh,' said the Elephant's Child. 'I don't think you peoples know anything about spanking; but I do, and I'll show you.'

Then he uncurled his trunk and knocked two of his dear brothers head over heels.

'O Bananas!' said they, 'where did you learn that trick, and what have you done to your nose?'

'I got a new one from the Crocodile on the banks of the great, grey-green, greasy Limpopo River,' said the Elephant's Child. 'I asked him what he had for dinner, and he gave me this to keep.'

'It looks very ugly,' said his hairy uncle, the Baboon.

'It does,' said the Elephant's Child. 'But it's very useful,' and he picked up his hairy uncle, the Baboon, by one hairy leg, and hove him into a hornet's nest.

Then that bad Elephant's Child spanked all his dear families for a long time, till they were very warm and greatly astonished. He pulled out his tall Ostrich aunt's tail-feathers; and he caught his tall uncle, the Giraffe, by the hind-leg, and dragged him through a thorn-bush; and he shouted at his broad aunt, the Hippopotamus, and blew bubbles into her ear when she was sleeping in the water after meals; but he never let anyone touch Kolokolo Bird.

At last things grew so exciting that his dear families went off one by one in a hurry to the banks of the great, grey-green, greasy Limpopo River, all set about with fever-trees, to borrow new noses from the Crocodile. When they came back nobody spanked anybody any more, and ever since that day, O Best Beloved, all the Elephants you will ever see, besides all those that you won't, have trunks precisely like the trunk of the 'satiable Elephant's Child.

Persephone

This is a story of a girl with a name like music, Persephone. She was the Greek goddess of the spring. Lambs frisked for her and calves gambolled for her; doves cooed to her and trees put on bright green leaves to welcome her. Flowers opened their buds to call, 'Persephone', and the green grass waved and whispered, 'Persephone'.

Her mother, Demeter, was goddess of the cornfields. She was tall and stately and queenly, but when she smiled she looked so kind and comfortable that all the little children forgot she was a goddess and wanted to climb into her lap and kiss her. The fields loved her so much that everywhere she went the corn grew tall and ripened to the harvest; so everyone called her 'Corn-mother Demeter'.

One morning Persephone said to her mother, 'I am going to climb the mountain today with my friends. We want to pick flowers to thread into necklaces.'

'Do not climb too high,' answered Demeter; 'you can easily get lost on the mountain. Take some milk and honey-cakes with you; you have time to milk the black goat.'

So Persephone took some honey-cakes and a jar of milk and skipped out to join her friends. She met them in an orchard, and the pear-trees opened their white blossom to welcome her. Laughing and talking,

Persephone and her friends climbed the hill. They walked beneath silvery trees and between sweet-smelling bushes. They climbed on and on till they were high up on grassy slopes, with rocky walls above them. Everywhere the green grass waved and whispered, 'Persephone', and everywhere the flowers opened their buds to call, 'Persephone'. Soon the whole hillside was bright with flowers.

Persephone and her friends were so excited that they ran from one clump of flowers to another. They picked a few here and ran on and picked a few there. There was always another even lovelier clump farther on.

At last they began to feel hungry. So they sat down in a green hollow among sweet-smelling bushes to eat their honey-cakes and drink the black goat's milk.

When they had finished they started to thread the flowers into necklaces. They had picked little anemones with black eyes and silky red petals. They had starry blue speedwell and yellow narcissus, baby sweet-peas and tiny snap-dragon. They made lovely necklaces. Persephone had nearly finished hers and was trying it round her neck to see if it was long enough, when there came a jarring, gnarring, krarring, 'crrrrrack'.

'Crrrrrack!' It sounded as if the rocky walls above them had split right open. The hillside had split open, and out of a great crack in the side of the mountain galloped four splendid black horses.

The four black horses pulled a golden chariot, and in the golden chariot stood a great black-bearded king. In his right hand he carried a key, and with his left hand he shook the reins furiously. This was Pluto,

King of the Caves and Caverns, King of the world Underground, god of the Underworld.

Pluto shook his reins furiously and drove straight toward Persephone. She jumped up, and her friends jumped up, so frightened that they spilt all their flowers on the ground. Then they scattered in all directions but while her friends escaped, the four great black horses galloped straight toward Persephone.

Persephone screamed, 'Mother, Cornmother, help!'

But Pluto leant right out of his golden chariot and caught her by the waist and swung her up beside him.

Persephone was so frightened that she cried bitterly. Pluto, King of the Underworld, tried to comfort her; he said, 'I am Pluto, King of the Caves and Caverns. We shall live in the world underground and there you shall be my Queen.'

But Persephone called, 'Mother, Cornmother, help!' and cried bitterly.

Pluto pulled at the reins of his four black horses and swung round the chariot. He galloped his horses furiously back toward the caves and caverns. They galloped into the gap in the mountainside, and the rock wall closed behind them with a jarring, gnarring, krarring, 'crrrrrack'. Pluto and Persephone had vanished into the Underworld; only her flowers were left outside.

All this time Demeter was far away. She was walking through the cornfields with a basket in her hand, helping the corn to grow tall and ripen to the harvest. When she heard a far-off crying, like a faint, faint echo, she thought, 'That is Persephone.' So she began to run toward the mountain.

Cornmother Demeter ran through the orchards and beneath the silvery trees. She climbed up on to the grassy slopes, calling, 'Persephone, Persephone.' She thought, 'I can easily find her; the flowers will have opened their buds for her, and they will show me which way she went.'

But flowers no longer sprang up on the hillside. Yellow narcissi and silky red anemones, baby sweet-peas and tiny snap-dragons, all had closed their buds and bent their heads. She ran here and there and everywhere, calling, 'Persephone,' and the rocky walls echoed back, 'Persephone.'

Cornmother Demeter looked and looked for her daughter. The sun went down and the stars came out, one by one. The moon climbed into the sky, and the grass turned silvery in the moonbeams. She searched all night, calling, 'Persephone.' Very early in the morning she found the necklaces of withered flowers.

Demeter went on searching. She scrambled all over the mountain and climbed to the very top of it. She searched fields and woods, orchards and gardens. She asked everyone, 'Have you seen Persephone?' But her friends had run far away, and no one had seen her.

At last the sun god took pity on the Queen of the Cornfields. He came down out of the sky and said, 'Pluto, god of the Underworld, has carried her away.'

Demeter wept bitterly because she thought that she might never see Persephone again. Then she went away to a far country.

Persephone was sad in the Underworld. Pluto gave her a beautiful black dress; he hung necklaces of bright stones round her neck, he put rings in her ears and rings on her fingers, he covered her arms with bracelets and crowned her with a golden crown. Then he gave her a silver chair to sit in and piled delicious things to eat on golden dishes. He begged her to eat.

Persephone sat straight and still and she would not eat anything. She wanted Cornmother Demeter; and in the Underworld there was nothing to comfort her. There was no grass to wave and whisper, 'Persephone'; there were no flowers to open their buds and call, 'Persephone'.

Indeed, there were no longer any flowers in the world above, for Demeter and Persephone no longer walked through the orchards and fields. The leaves turned brown and fell off the trees; the grass turned yellow and withered away; the corn drooped and dried. Soon there was hardly any corn left to grind into flour and bake into bread. Everywhere children were crying because they were hungry.

Now, Zeus was King of all the gods. He spoke in a voice of thunder, and lightning flashed from his hand. He heard children crying, and he saw bare trees and brown fields, and he asked, 'Where is Demeter, Queen of the Cornfields?'

'In a far country,' answered the gods.

Zeus frowned terribly and sent his messenger to fetch Demeter. She came and stood before him, and she said, 'Tell Pluto to let Persephone come back from the Underworld. I will not help the corn to ripen to the harvest unless she walks through the fields beside me.'

All the children were crying louder than ever, and their fathers and mothers were crying too. So Zeus had pity on them and he sent a messenger to King Pluto, 'Give back Persephone to her mother.'

But Pluto loved Persephone too, and he could not bear to lose her. He did not know what to do; for Persephone would eat nothing in the Underworld, and unless she ate something he would have to obey Zeus and send her back to Cornmother Demeter.

Pluto was clever and cunning. He chose a pomegranate fruit, red and wrinkled and round like an apple. He cut it in half and it had golden juice and yellow seeds inside. He carried it to Persephone on a silver plate.

Pluto said to her, 'Zeus has ordered me to send you

back to your mother. Before you leave the Underworld show me that you do not hate me; be kind and eat this pomegranate for my sake.'

Pluto had given Persephone necklaces and bracelets, and he had put rings on her fingers and a crown on her head; she remembered that he had tried to be kind. So very slowly she picked up a spoon and put it in the pomegranate. Very, very slowly she put six pomegranate seeds into her mouth. She ate the six seeds. Then Pluto laughed happily and said, 'Now you cannot go back to your mother. You will have to stay for ever with me.'

When Zeus heard that Persephone had eaten pomegranate seeds, he said, 'Demeter, you must walk through the fields without Persephone. Now that she has eaten she cannot come back from the Underworld.'

But Demeter answered, 'I cannot help the corn to grow tall and ripen to the harvest without Persephone. I miss her so much and I am so unhappy.'

Fathers and mothers and children were crying so loudly that Zeus could not bear to hear them. 'Persephone has eaten in the Underworld,' he said, 'so I cannot take her right away from King Pluto. But she only ate six pomegranate seeds. For six months of the year, therefore, she shall be Queen in the Underworld, but for six months she shall walk through the fields and orchards with her mother, and the grass and the flowers and trees shall grow green again.'

When Persephone came up from the Underworld to meet her mother, the trees put on bright green leaves to welcome her. The flowers opened their buds to call, 'Persephone', and the grass turned green and waved and whispered, 'Persephone.' She walked through the fields with her mother and the corn grew under their feet. Spring had come back to the world. And so it is today. When Persephone goes down to the Under-world, trees shed their leaves and all the flowers die. Winter is here. But when she comes back, she brings spring with her; she brings daffodils and daisies and dandelions, and the corn grows green in the fields.

The Golden Touch

Once upon a time, there lived a very rich man, and a king besides, whose name was Midas: and he had a little daughter, whose name I never knew. So, because I love odd names for little girls, I choose to call her Marygold.

This King Midas was fonder of gold than of anything else in the world. If he loved anything better, or half so well, it was the one little maiden who played so merrily around her father's foot-stool. But the more Midas loved his daughter, the more did he desire and seek for wealth. He thought, foolish man! that the best thing he could possibly do for this dear child would be to leave her the immensest pile of yellow, glistening coin, that had ever been heaped together since the world was made. Thus he gave all his thoughts and all his time to this one purpose. If ever he happened to gaze for an instant at the gold-tinted clouds of sunset, he wished that they were real gold, and that they could be squeezed safely into his treasure-box. When little Marygold ran to meet him, with a bunch of buttercups and dandelions, he used to say: 'Pooh, pooh, child! If these were as golden as they look, they would be worth the gathering!'

And yet, in his earlier days, before he had this craving for gold, King Midas had shown a great taste for flowers. He had planted a garden, in which grew the biggest and beautifullest and sweetest roses that any mortal ever saw or smelt. These roses were still growing in the garden, as large, as lovely, and as fragrant as when Midas used to pass whole hours in gazing at them, and inhaling their perfume. But now, if he looked at them at all, it was only to work out how much the garden would be worth, if each of the innumerable rose-petals were a thin plate of gold. And though he once was fond of music, the only music for poor Midas now was the chink of one coin against another.

At length, Midas could scarcely bear to see or touch any object that was not gold. He made it his custom, therefore, to pass a large portion of every day in a dark and dreary room, underground, at the basement

of his palace. It was here that he kept his wealth. To this dismal hole – for it was little better than a dungeon – Midas took himself, whenever he wanted to be particularly happy. Here, after carefully locking the door, he would take a bag of gold coin, or a gold cup as big as a wash-bowl, or a heavy golden bar, or a peck-measure of gold-dust, and bring them from the dark corners of the room into the one bright sunbeam that fell from the dungeon-like window. He valued the sunbeam for no other reason but that this his treasure would not shine without its help. And then would he reckon over the coins in the bag; toss up the bar, and catch it as it came down; sift the gold-dust through his fingers; look at the funny image of his own face, as reflected in the burnished surface of the cup; and whisper to himself: 'O Midas, rich King Midas, what a happy man thou art!' But it was laughable to see how the image of his face kept grinning at him. It seemed to be aware of his foolish behaviour and to have a naughty desire to make fun of him.

Midas called himself a happy man, but felt that he was not yet quite so happy as he might be. The very tiptop of enjoyment would never be reached unless the whole world were to become his treasure-room and be filled with yellow metal which should be all his own.

Now, I need hardly remind such wise little people as you are that in the old, old times, when King Midas was alive, a great many things came to pass which we should consider wonderful if they were to happen in our own day and country.

Midas was enjoying himself in his treasure-room,

one day, as usual, when he noticed a shadow fall over the heaps of gold; and, looking suddenly up, what should be behold but the figure of a stranger, standing in the bright and narrow sunbeam! It was a young man, with a cheerful and ruddy face. Midas could not help fancying that the smile with which the stranger looked at him had a kind of golden radiance in it. Certainly he now saw a brighter gleam upon all his piled-up treasures than before. Even the remotest corners were lighted up when the stranger smiled, as with tips of flame and sparkles of fire.

As Midas knew that he had carefully turned the key in the lock, and that no mortal strength could possibly break into his treasure-room, he, of course, concluded that his visitor must be something more than mortal. The stranger, indeed, looked so good-humoured and kindly, that it did not seem right to suspect him of intending any mischief. It was far more probable that he came to do Midas a favour.

The stranger gazed about the room; and when his lustrous smile had glistened upon all the golden objects that were there, he turned again to Midas.

'You are a wealthy man, friend Midas!' he observed. 'I doubt whether any other four walls on earth contain so much gold as you will have piled up in this room.'

'I have done pretty well – pretty well,' answered Midas in a discontented tone. 'But, after all, it is but little when you consider that it has taken me my whole life to get it together. If only I could live for a thousand years, then I might have time to grow really rich!'

'What!' exclaimed the stranger. 'Then you are not satisfied?'

Midas shook his head.

'And pray what would satisfy you?' asked the stranger.

Midas paused and thought. He thought, and thought, and thought. At last, a bright idea occurred to King Midas.

Raising his head he looked the lustrous stranger in the face.

'Well, Midas,' observed the visitor, 'I see that you have at length hit upon something that will satisfy you. Tell me your wish.'

'It is only this,' replied Midas. 'I am weary of collecting my treasures with so much trouble, and seeing the heap so tiny after I have done my best. I wish everything that I touch to be changed to gold!'

'The Golden Touch!' exclaimed he. 'You certainly deserve credit, friend Midas, for so brilliant an idea. But are you quite sure that this will satisfy you?'

'How could it fail!' said Midas.

'And will you never regret the possession of it?'

'I ask for nothing else to render me perfectly happy,' answered Midas.

'Be it as you wish, then,' replied the stranger. 'Tomorrow, at sunrise, you will find yourself gifted with the Golden Touch.'

The figure of the stranger then became exceedingly bright, and Midas had to close his eyes. On opening them again, he beheld only one yellow sunbeam in the room, and, all around him, the glistening of the

precious metal which he had spent his life in hoarding
up.

Whether Midas slept as usual that night the story
does not say. Asleep or awake, however, his mind was
probably like that of a child to whom a beautiful new
plaything has been promised in the morning. At any
rate, day had hardly peeped over the hills, when King
Midas was broad awake, and, stretching his arms out
of bed, began to touch the objects that were within
reach. He was anxious to prove whether the Golden
Touch had really come, according to the stranger's
promise. So he laid his finger on a chair by the bedside, and on various other things, but was grievously
disappointed to see that they remained exactly as
before. Indeed, he felt very much afraid that he had
only dreamed about the lustrous stranger. And what a
miserable affair would it be, if, after all his hopes,
Midas must content himself with what little gold he
could scrape together by ordinary means, instead of
creating it by a touch!

All this while it was only the grey of the morning,
with only a streak of brightness along the edge of the
sky. Midas, lay, getting moodier each minute as he
saw his hopes fading, and kept growing sadder and
sadder, until the earliest sunbeam shone through the
window, and gilded the ceiling over his head. It
seemed to Midas that this bright yellow sunbeam was
reflected on the white covering of the bed. Looking
more closely, what was his astonishment and delight,
when he found that his bed-cover had turned into a
cloth of the purest and brightest gold! The Golden

Touch had come to him, with the first sunbeam!

Midas started up, in a kind of joyful frenzy, and ran about the room grasping at everything that happened to be in his way. He seized one of the bedposts and it became immediately a golden pillar. He pulled aside a window curtain and the tassel grew heavy in his hand – a mass of gold. He hurriedly put on his clothes, and was enraptured to see himself in a magnificent suit of gold cloth. He drew out his handkerchief, which little Marygold had hemmed for him. That was likewise gold, with the dear child's neat and pretty stitches running all along the border, in gold thread!

Somehow or other, this last transformation did not quite please King Midas. He would rather that his little daughter's handiwork should have remained just the same as when she climbed his knee and put it into his hand.

But it was not worth while to vex himself about so small a matter. Midas now took his spectacles from his pocket, and put them on his nose, in order that he might see more distinctly what he was about. To his great perplexity, however, he discovered that he could not possibly see through them. But this was the most natural thing in the world; for, on taking them off, the transparent glass turned out to be plates of gold and were now quite useless as spectacles. It struck Midas as rather inconvenient. 'It is no great matter, nevertheless,' said he to himself, very philosophically. 'We cannot expect any great good without its being accompanied by some small inconvenience. The

Golden Touch is worth the sacrifice of a pair of spectacles at the very least.'

King Midas now went downstairs, and smiled, on observing that the banister became a bar of burnished gold, as his hand passed over it. He lifted the door latch, which turned golden at the touch of his fingers, and went into the garden. Here, as it happened, he found a great number of beautiful roses in full bloom, and others in all the stages of lovely bud and blossom. Very delicious was their fragrance in the morning breeze. Their delicate blush was one of the fairest sights in the world; so gentle, and so full of sweet tranquillity did these roses seem to be.

But Midas knew a way to make them far more precious, according to his way of thinking, than roses had ever been before. So he rushed from bush to bush, touching the roses until every individual flower and bud, and even the worms at the heart of some of them, were changed to gold. By the time this good work was completed, King Midas was called to breakfast; and, as the morning air had given him an excellent appetite, he made haste back to the palace.

The breakfast consisted of hot cakes, some nice little brook trout, roasted potatoes, fresh boiled eggs, coffee for King Midas himself, and a bowl of bread and milk for his daughter, Marygold.

Little Marygold had not yet made her appearance. Her father ordered her to be called, and, seating himself at table, awaited the child's coming in order to begin his own breakfast. It was not a great while before he heard her coming along the passage, crying bitterly. This surprised Midas, because Marygold was one of the cheerfullest little people whom you would see in a summer's day, and hardly shed a thimbleful of tears in a twelvemonth. When Midas heard her sobs, he determined to make his little Marygold happier by giving her a pleasant surprise; so, leaning across the table, he touched his daughter's bowl (which was a china one, with pretty figures all around it), and changed it to gleaming gold.

Meanwhile, Marygold slowly opened the door, and showed herself with her apron at her eyes, still sobbing as if her heart would break.

'How now, my little lady?' cried Midas. 'Pray what is the matter with you this bright morning?'

Marygold, without taking the apron from her eyes, held out her hand, in which was one of the roses Midas had so recently changed to gold.

'Beautiful!' exclaimed her father. 'And what is there in this magnificent golden rose to make you cry?'

'Ah, dear father!' answered the child, as well as her sobs would let her; 'it is not beautiful, but the ugliest flower that ever grew! As soon as I was dressed, I ran into the garden to gather some roses for you; because I know you like them, and like them better when gathered by your little daughter. But, oh dear, dear me! What do you think has happened? Such a misfortune! All the beautiful roses, that smelled so sweetly and had so many lovely blushes, are blighted and spoilt! They are grown quite yellow, as you see this one, and have no longer any perfume! What can be the matter with them?'

'Pooh, my dear little girl – pray don't cry about it!' said Midas, who was ashamed to confess that he himself had brought about the change which so greatly saddened her. 'Sit down and eat your bread and milk! A golden rose like that will last hundreds of years and you would find it easy enough to exchange it for an ordinary one, which would wither in a day.'

'I don't care for such roses as this!' cried Marygold, tossing it away. 'It has no smell, and the hard petals prick my nose!'

The child now sat down to table, but was so occupied with her sadness for the blighted roses that she did not even notice the wonderful change of her china bowl. Perhaps this was all the better; for Marygold loved to look at the queer figures and strange trees and houses, that were painted on the bowl; and these were now entirely lost in the gold of the metal.

Midas, meanwhile, lifted a spoonful of coffee to his lips, and, sipping it, was astonished to find that, the instant his lips touched the liquid, it became molten gold, and, the next moment, hardened into a lump!

'Ha!' exclaimed Midas, rather aghast.

'What is the matter, father?' asked little Marygold, gazing at him with the tears still standing in her eyes.

'Nothing, child, nothing!' said Midas. 'Have your milk, before it gets quite cold.'

He took one of the nice little trouts on his plate, and, by way of experiment, touched its tail with his finger. To his horror, it was immediately changed from an admirably fried brook trout into a fish of gold. Its little bones were now golden wires; its fins and tail were thin plates of gold; and there were marks of the fork in it, exactly imitated in metal. A very pretty piece of work, as you may suppose; only King Midas, just at that moment, would much rather have had a real trout in his dish.

'I don't quite see,' thought he to himself, 'how I am to get any breakfast!'

He took one of the smoking hot cakes, and had scarcely broken it, when it, too, turned to gold. Almost in despair, he helped himself to a boiled egg, which immediately underwent a change similar to those of the trout and the cake.

'Well, this is a quandary!' thought he, leaning back in his chair and looking quite enviously at little Marygold, who was now eating her bread and milk with great satisfaction. 'Such a costly breakfast before me, and nothing that can be eaten!'

King Midas next snatched a hot potato, and attempted to cram it into his mouth, and swallow it in a hurry. But the Golden Touch was too nimble for him. He found his mouth full, not of mealy potato, but of solid metal, which so burnt his tongue that he roared aloud, and, jumping up from the table, began to dance and stamp about the room, both with pain and fright.

'Father, dear father!' cried little Marygold, who was a very affectionate child, 'pray what is the matter? Have you burnt your mouth?'

'Ah, dear child,' groaned Midas miserably, 'I don't know what is to become of your poor father!'

And, truly, my dear little folks, did you ever hear of such a pitiable case in all your lives? Here was literally the richest breakfast that could be set before a king, yet the poorest labourer, sitting down to his crust of bread and cup of water, was far better off than King Midas, at this moment. And what was to be done? Already, at breakfast, Midas was excessively hungry. Would it, he wondered, be the same at dinner-time? And how ravenous would be his appetite for supper? How was he going to live if all his food changed to gold?

So great was his hunger, and the perplexity of his situation, that he again groaned aloud, and very piteously too. Our pretty Marygold could endure it no longer. She sat a moment gazing at her father, and trying, with all the might of her little wits, to find out what was the matter with him. Then, with a sweet and sorrowful impulse to comfort him, she darted from her chair, and running to Midas, threw her arms affectionately about his neck. He bent down and kissed her. He felt that his little daughter's love was worth a thousand times more than all he had gained by the Golden Touch.

'My precious, precious Marygold!' cried he.

But Marygold made no answer.

Alas, what had he done? How fatal was the gift the stranger had granted him! The moment the lips of Midas touched Marygold's forehead, a change had taken place. Her sweet, rosy face, so full of affection as it had been, took on a glittering yellow colour, with yellow tear-drops hardening on her cheeks. Her beautiful brown ringlets hung stiffly about her face. Her soft and tender little body grew hard and stiff in her father's arms. Oh, terrible misfortune! Little Marygold was a human child no longer, but a golden statue!

Yes, there she was, with the questioning look of love, and pity hardened into her face. It was the prettiest and most sorrowful sight that ever mortal saw. All the features of Marygold were there; even the beloved little dimple remained in her golden chin. Now, when it was too late, he felt how much more precious was a warm and tender heart, that loved him, than all the gold in the world.

Midas began to wring his hands and moan, and now he could neither bear to look at Marygold, nor yet to look away from her. He could not possibly believe that she was changed to gold. But there was the precious little figure, with a yellow teardrop on its yellow cheek, and a look so piteous and tender that it seemed as if that very expression should soften the gold, and make it flesh again. This, however, could not be. So Midas could only wring his hands and wish that he was the poorest man in the wide world, if the loss of all his wealth might bring back the faintest rose-colour to his dear child's face.

While he was in this state of blank despair, he suddenly beheld a stranger standing near the door. Midas bent down his head, without speaking; for he recognized the same figure which had appeared to him the day before in the treasure-room, and had granted him the disastrous Golden Touch.

'Well, friend Midas,' said the stranger, 'pray how are you enjoying the Golden Touch?'

Midas shook his head.

'I am very miserable,' said he.

'Very miserable, indeed!' exclaimed the stranger. 'And how does that come to be? Have I not faithfully kept my promise with you? Have you not everything that your heart desired?'

'Gold is not everything,' answered Midas. 'And I have lost all that my heart really cared for.'

'Ah! So you have made a discovery since yesterday?' observed the stranger. 'Let us see, then. Which of these two things do you think is really worth the most – the gift of the Golden Touch, or one cup of clear cold water?'

'Oh, blessed water!' exclaimed Midas. 'It will never moisten my parched throat again!'

'The Golden Touch,' continued the stranger, 'or a crust of bread?'

'A piece of bread,' answered Midas, 'is worth all the gold on earth!'

'The Golden Touch,' asked the stranger, 'or your own little Marygold, warm, soft, and loving as she was an hour ago?'

'Oh, my child, my dear child!' cried poor Midas, wringing his hands. 'I would not have given that one small dimple in her chin for the power of changing this whole big earth into a solid lump of gold!'

'You are wiser than you were, King Midas,' said the stranger, looking seriously at him. 'Your own heart, I see, has not been entirely changed from flesh to gold.

You appear now to understand that the commonest things, such as lie within everybody's grasp, are more precious than all the riches you have been sighing for all these years. Tell me, now, do you sincerely desire to rid yourself of this Golden Touch?'

'It is hateful to me,' replied Midas.

A fly settled on his nose, but immediately fell to the floor; for it, too, had become gold. Midas shuddered.

'Go, then,' said the stranger, 'and plunge into the river that glides past the bottom of your garden. Take also a vase of the same water, and sprinkle it over any object that you wish to change back again from gold into its former substance.'

King Midas bowed low; and when he lifted his head, the lustrous stranger had vanished.

You will easily believe that Midas lost no time in snatching up a great earthen pitcher and hastening to the river-side. On reaching the river's brink, he plunged headlong in, without waiting so much as to pull off his shoes.

'Poof! Poof! Poof!' snorted King Midas, as his head emerged out of the water. 'Well, this is really a refreshing bath, and I think it must have quite washed away the Golden Touch. And now for filling my pitcher!'

As he dipped the pitcher into the water, it gladdened his very heart to see it change from gold into the same good, honest, earthen vessel which it had been before. He also felt some change within himself. A cold, hard, and heavy weight seemed to have gone from him and he felt light and happy. No doubt his heart had been changing to gold but had now softened again and had become gentle and kind. Noticing a violet that grew on the bank of the river, Midas touched it with his finger, and was overjoyed to find that the delicate flower kept its purple colour, instead of undergoing a change to gold. The curse of the Golden Touch had really been removed from him.

King Midas hastened back to the palace, carefully bringing home the earthen pitcher of water: that water, which was to undo all the mischief that his foolishness had brought about was more precious to Midas than an ocean of molten gold could have been. The first thing he did, as you need hardly be told, was to sprinkle it by handfuls over the golden figure of little Marygold.

You would have laughed to see how the rosy colour came back to the dear child's cheeks and she began to sneeze and splutter; and how astonished she was to find herself dripping wet, and her father still throwing more water over her!

'Pray do not, dear father!' cried she. 'See how you have wet my nice frock, which I put on only this morning!'

For Marygold did not know that she had been a little golden statue; nor could she remember anything that had happened since the moment when she ran, with outstretched arms, to comfort poor King Midas.

Her father did not think it necessary to tell his beloved child how very foolish he had been, but contented himself with showing how much wiser he had grown. For this purpose he led little Marygold into the garden, where he sprinkled all the remainder of the water over the rose-bushes and instantly thousands of roses recovered their beautiful bloom.

There were two things, however, which, as long as he lived, used to put King Midas in mind of the Golden Touch. One was, that the sands of the river sparkled like gold; the other, that little Marygold's hair had now a golden tinge, which he had never seen in it before she had been changed by the effect of his kiss.

When King Midas had grown quite an old man, and used to trot Marygold's children on his knee, he was fond of telling them this marvellous story, pretty much as I have now told it to you. And then he would stroke their glossy ringlets, and tell them that their hair, likewise, had the same rich shade of gold. 'And, to tell you the truth, my precious little folks,' King Midas would say to them, 'ever since that morning, I have hated the very sight of all other gold, but this!'

Acknowledgements

We are most grateful to the undermentioned publishers and authors for permission to include the following stories:

Messrs J. M. Dent & Sons for *The Golden Touch* (adapted from Nathaniel Hawthorne's version).

The Literary Trustees of Walter de la Mare and the Society of Authors as their representatives for *The Hare and the Hedgehog* and *The Grateful Beasts*, from *Animal Stories*, published by Faber & Faber Ltd.

Messrs A. & C. Black for *The Giant with the Three Golden Hairs* (from *Grimms' Fairy Tales*).

Messrs Coward-McCann Inc., New York, for *Spindle, Shuttle and Needle* from *Tales from Grimm* by Wanda Gág (published in Britain by Faber & Faber Ltd).

Messrs Thomas Nelson & Sons Ltd, and Mr Arthur Ransome for *Baba Yaga and the Little Girl with the Kind Heart*.

Messrs Macmillan and the Macmillan Company and Mrs George Bambridge for *The Elephant's Child* by Rudyard Kipling (from *Just So Stories*).

V. H. Drummond (V. H. Drummond Productions Ltd) for *The Flying Postman*.

The Oxford University Press for *East of the Sun and West of the Moon* (from *Scandinavian Legends* by Gwyn Jones).

The Oxford University Press for *Persephone* (from *Classical Stories* by Freda Saxey. Reprinted by permission of the publishers).

The Society of Authors as the literary representatives of the estate of the late Rose Fyleman for *The Three Dogs*.

Acknowledgements

Messrs Frederick Muller for *The Three Sillies* (from *English Fairy Tales*, collected and adapted by Joseph Jacobs).

Messrs Faber & Faber Ltd for *The Tinder Box* and *The Ugly Duckling* by Hans Andersen (translated by M. R. James).

We should also like to record our gratitude to Miss Eileen H. Colwell, and Miss Phyllis Hunt of Faber & Faber for help and advice at all times.

Some other Young Puffins

MR BERRY'S ICE CREAM PARLOUR
Jennifer Zabel

Carl is thrilled when Mr Berry, the new lodger, comes to stay. But when Mr Berry announces his plan to open an ice-cream parlour, Carl can hardly believe it. And this is just the start of the excitements in store when Mr Berry walks through the door!

THE RAILWAY CAT AND DIGBY
Phyllis Arkle

Further adventures of Alfie, the Railway Cat, who always seems to be in Leading Railman Hack's bad books. Alfie is a smart cat, a lot smarter than many people think, and he would like to be friends with Hack. But when he tries to improve matters, by 'helping' Hack's dog, Digby, win a prize at the local show, the situation rapidly goes from bad to worse!'

THE BUREAUCATS
Richard Adams

Imagine events in a large household, seen through the eyes of Richard and Thomas Kitten, who feel life should be organized entirely around them – it isn't of course, and the consequences are highly entertaining.

MY FIRST BIG STORY BOOK
MY SECOND BIG STORY BOOK
MY THIRD BIG STORY BOOK

ed. Richard Bamberger

A bottomless well of folktales and fables to fill odd moments or long rainy afternoons.

BAD BOYS

ed. Eileen Colwell

A round dozen stories, with some rhymes as well, but all of them about naughty boys.

THE PICTURE PRIZE

Simon Watson

An enchanting collection of fifteen fresh and amusing stories about mischievous Wallace and his younger brother, Henry. From unexpected pony rides to collecting caterpillars, to losing a tooth, it's clear that everyday incidents become real adventures when Wallace is around!

TALES FROM ALLOTMENT LANE SCHOOL

Margaret Joy

A collection of twelve lively stories set in the reception class of a primary school. Miss Mee and her mixed class of five-year-olds have a series of day-to-day experiences, which make extremely entertaining and humorous reading.

THE DISAPPEARING CAT and NO SWIMMING FOR SAM

Thelma Lambert

Two stories about school life, appearing together in one volume for the first time.

THE THREE AND MANY WISHES OF JASON REID

Hazel Hutchins

Eleven-year-old Jason is a very good thinker. So when Quicksilver (no more than eighteen inches high) grants him three wishes, he's extremely wary. After all, in fairy tales, this kind of thing always leads to disaster. So Jason is absolutely determined to get *his* wishes right. But it's not that easy, and he lands himself and his friends in all sorts of terrible but funny scrapes!